F ARMSTRONG
Armstrong, Kelley
Brazen

D0597083

BRAZEN

FOUNTAINDALE PUBLIC LIBRARY DISTRICT
300 West Briarcliff Road
Bolingbrook, IL 60440-2894
(630) 759-2102

BRAZEN

Kelley Armstrong

ILLUSTRATIONS BY XAVIÈRE DAUMARIE

SUBTERRANEAN PRESS 2013

Brazen Copyright © 2013 by KLA Fricke Inc.
All rights reserved.

Dust jacket and interior illustrations Copyright © 2013
by Xavière Daumarie. All rights reserved.

Interior design Copyright © 2013 Desert Isle Design, LLC.
All rights reserved.

First Edition

ISBN
978-1-59606-616-8

Subterranean Press
PO Box 190106
Burton, MI 48519

subterraneanpress.com

One

NICK

WHEN NICK SORRENTINO'S alarm went off at five a.m., he bolted upright, certain it was his phone ringing, some emergency unfolding. Five years ago, he would have figured it'd be Elena or Clay with a Pack problem. These days, his first thought was "the boys." Reese or Noah was in trouble and needed his help. Or had been out drinking and needed a lift. Even with werewolves, the second was more likely, particularly if the werewolves in question were twenty-two and nineteen.

But it wasn't his phone ringing—it was the alarm. Why the hell would he set it for five a.m.? It must have been one of the boys, playing a sadistic...

As he reached to shut the phone off, he was stopped by the fact it was not on the nightstand beside him. Well, yes, it was, but there was an obstacle in between. A woman.

She groaned, fumbled for his phone and handed it to him.

Right. That was why he'd set the alarm. He needed to get home to take Noah to school because he'd been grounded from using his car, which was, Nick had to admit, turning out to be more of a punishment for him than for Noah.

At least he'd had the presence of mind to set the alarm. That alone was an accomplishment, given that he'd realized he *wasn't* heading home while in the back of a cab as Jacinda undid his zipper. Damn lucky he'd remembered. Or perhaps, he mused, a sign that he'd really had one too many women go down on him in the back of a taxi if he could still think "Huh, I should set my alarm." That, or he was getting old.

"Are you going to turn that off?" said a voice.

It was a woman's voice. But it didn't come from Jacinda's side of the bed. Nick looked over to see her friend, Heidi, curled up on his other side. Right. Huh. Well, maybe he wasn't that old yet.

He shut off his alarm. Then he checked his e-mail, making sure he didn't have an angry one from Frank Russell. Russell was a client he'd taken out last night on a double-date with Jacinda and her friend. Nick looked from Jacinda to Heidi.

Not the way a double-date was supposed to work. But in Nick's world, they did seem to, with rather alarming frequency.

He did have an e-mail from Russell, but only thanking him for the evening out, and asking if he had Heidi's phone number. According to Russell, they'd left together, then she'd had some emergency and taken off. Which was when she'd hopped into the cab with Nick and Jacinda, just before it pulled away from the curb. From there, well, things escalated. At least Russell hadn't figured it out.

Nick climbed over Jacinda and started pulling on his trousers. Heidi rolled from bed and stumbled into the bathroom.

"Where are you rushing off to?" Jacinda asked as she watched him dress. "Your car is only ten minutes away, and you never start work before nine, which means we have plenty of time for another round. Or two."

She tugged down the covers, showing him what was on offer. It was, he had to admit, a very nice offer. Tempting, though? Well, that was the problem. Ten years ago, he would have already been back in that bed. Hell, he wouldn't have gotten *out* of it until he made sure they both started the day off right. Now, though, he stood there enjoying the sight of her, feeling an answering twitch in his groin and a spark of regret. But that was it.

"I'd love to," he said. "But I need to take Noah to school, and it's an hour drive home."

"The kid has his license, Nick. He even has a car."

"He lost his privileges for driving home after having a beer."

"A beer? One?"

Nick pulled on his shirt. "That's the rule."

"Since when do you follow rules?"

Since always, he could say. Maybe not the ones society set out for him—grow up, get a job, marry, have kids—but otherwise, rule-following was in his blood. He followed those rules of his kind, of his Pack, and imposing them on Noah was as important as sticking to them himself, no matter how inconvenient. Noah needed that stability more than most.

"I set out the punishment, I need to follow through with it."

Jacinda shook her head. "I'm not sure I like this new Nick. The old, irresponsible one was a whole lot more fun."

"Could have sworn you had fun last night. Or maybe that was just Heidi."

She smiled. "Okay, you're still fun that way. But taking in these cousins? And going to work every day? That's not the Nick I knew."

"I haven't been that Nick in years, Jace."

"I know, but it's getting worse. How long has it been since you called me? Two months? I'm beginning to think I might need to bring a friend more often, just to keep you interested."

He walked over and bent to kiss her. "You know better than that. Adding Heidi to the mix was your idea. I'm just flexible and accommodating."

"You are indeed."

She caught his hand and pulled him closer. Her other hand went to his waistband, but he peeled her fingers off.

"Don't tempt me, Jace. I really do need to leave."

He gave her a last quick kiss and started for the door.

"Were you even planning to come back?" she asked.

He glanced over his shoulder at her.

"Last night," she said. "Before I jumped you in the cab, were you even planning to come back to my place?"

"If you wanted me to," he said, which was the truth, even if it didn't quite answer the question. "Get some more sleep. I'll call you."

"Soon?"

He hesitated. He could lie and say yes. Most guys would. But that was never how he'd done things. Don't take her number if you won't call. Don't say you'll call if you don't plan to. Don't say it'll be soon if it won't be.

"I'll call when I can," he said and slipped out the door.

● ● ●

As Nick drove home, he left a message with his admin assistant to say he might be late. He worked for his father at the family business, which just happened to be a multinational corporation. Nick's corner of it was small, by choice. There was no way in hell he could run a business like that—he had neither the aptitude nor the interest. His realm was advertising. He wasn't even the boss there—again, not his thing.

His niche was graphic design and client services. He had an eye for what worked, whether it was clothing or advertisements. He also had an unerring instinct for knowing what people wanted. It wasn't a cut-throat ability to pander and manipulate, but a genuine desire to please.

When he disconnected, he received a text message for an entirely different sort of business. Pack business.

Nine months ago, Elena and Clay had discovered that a long-dead member was actually very much alive. At the same time, Elena had become Pack Alpha, with Clay as her beta. Between shifting Pack dynamics, regular Pack business and raising six-year-old twins, they had little time to search for Malcolm. Nick had offered to do it.

Malcolm Danvers. Father of Jeremy Danvers, the former Alpha. Nick remembered him well. Well and not fondly. No one remembered Malcolm fondly. They weren't searching to welcome him back. They were searching to kill him. Preferably before Jeremy found out he'd still been alive.

Werewolves were, by nature, violent sons of bitches, as Clay would say. Clay had been bitten at the age of five, rescued and brought home by Jeremy. The first time Nick met him, Clay knocked him flying. His way of saying hello. And establishing dominance. That's the way things worked in their world.

Nick didn't have much use for dominance. He was happier obeying orders than giving them. Except now that his best friends led the Pack and there was a younger generation to care for, he'd realized it was time for him to step up. Hence offering to handle the hunt for Malcolm.

Back to werewolves and violence, though. While Nick was a fine fighter, he didn't feel the usual drive to hunt, to protect territory, to fight for his place. Elena teased he satisfied that urge in his romantic pursuits, but the truth was, he didn't really pursue there either. Like hunting, he enjoyed it and he'd rarely turn down an opportunity, but it wasn't a driving force in his life.

Malcolm sat at the opposite end of the spectrum. He pursued fights and women with equal vigor, as Nick recalled. And with the same ferocity. Women were prizes to be conquered and then discarded. Or worse. Nick's grandfather, Dominic, had believed Malcolm killed Jeremy's mother. Not that the old Alpha had turned him out of the Pack for it. Malcolm was too good a fighter to lose over a dead woman. Another Pack, another time.

But now, Malcolm was back. And finding him was Nick's job.

Two

NICK

NICK LEFT HIS car in the drive. He'd drop Noah off, then come back and clean up for work. Before he headed in, he texted a reply on the Malcolm issue. He sent a second text as he reached the front porch. This one didn't have far to go—less than a hundred feet, he'd guess. To Noah. Asking if he was ready. He could just open the front door and holler, but these days, text messaging seemed the way to go, even within the walls of your own house. Given that the walls of that house encompassed ten thousand square feet of living space on a hundred-acre lot, Nick had to admit that hollering from the front door wasn't practical, no matter how good a werewolf's hearing.

The estate was sixty miles north of New York. A property that size within commuting distance did bring the occasional enterprising real estate agent to the gate on behalf of some billionaire or other. You had to be a billionaire to afford property like this. Or you had to have family who'd bought it three hundred years ago when they emigrated from Italy. The house had been rebuilt twice in the interim, but it was an ancestral home. A communal home, too. That was how werewolves lived, all generations under one roof. For years it had been just Nick and Antonio. Now there were the boys.

Reese and Noah were permanent residents. A third young werewolf—Morgan Walsh—was older than the other two, and even more skittish about settling into someone else's home. He was on one of his walkabouts, gone to stay with the Russian Pack for a few months. He'd be back, though, and was already hinting about finding work in New York and "renting" a room at the house. Rent wasn't necessary, but if it made Morgan feel less awkward about the situation, they'd take it. Young werewolves needed a Pack, but they needed a family and a home at least as much.

When Nick opened the door, Reese greeted him. Coffee in hand, bleary eyed, he looked as if he hadn't gotten a moment's sleep. Which he hadn't. He'd just returned after a night shift at one of the family factories. His

choice—Antonio certainly wouldn't make his dependents work for a living, as Nick well knew. Reese was studying for his MBA and in the meantime he wanted to learn the business from the ground up. Which included working night shift at a factory.

The young Australian needed to feel like he was pulling his weight. Part of that was the werewolf in him, wanting to take a full role in his Pack. Part of it was just Reese. Nick didn't interfere, even if he would like to see the young man cut loose now and then.

"Thank you," Nick said, plucking the coffee from Reese's hand.

"Um, that was mine."

"I know. But you should be heading to bed, which means you do not need caffeine. I do." Nick leaned into the next room. "Noah!"

"He's coming. Slowly, as usual. He said you stayed in the city. You should have texted me. I'd have given him a lift to school. No need to end your date early."

"I had to come home and change anyway."

Reese lifted one eyebrow. "Um, no. You keep a bag in your car."

"I took it out last time we went to Stonehaven."

"That was a month ago."

Nick shrugged. "I forgot to put it back in."

Reese stared as if Nick had left behind his cell phone for a month. As Nick walked into the kitchen Noah swung around the corner, running his hand through his hair. That, along with brushing his teeth, constituted his idea of proper grooming. Sometimes Nick swore he did it just because it made Nick shudder.

"Are we shaving today?" Nick asked as Noah grabbed an apple.

"You can. I've got another day."

Nick couldn't argue. Noah did only need it a few times a week. He didn't look nineteen. Or eighteen, which was his official age, having shaved off a year when they'd taken him in, to help him catch up, academically and otherwise.

Nick could say Noah just took after his father. Joey Stillwell had grown up with Nick and Clay, and he'd always been small, always looked young, even for a werewolf. With Noah, though...well, there were other problems. Namely an alcoholic mother who hadn't stopped drinking during her pregnancy. Add in a rough life with a brutal stepdad and Joey almost out of the picture, and you ended up with a whole slew of issues, from delayed maturity to learning problems to a hair-trigger temper. The last two had much improved since Noah came to live with them, but there was nothing that could be done about the first. At least he'd finally started his Changes a few months ago, which helped.

"So I guess your date went well," Noah said, brows waggling as he took a bite of his apple.

"Do Nick's dates ever not go well?" Reese said, reaching for a banana. "So how about Russell's?"

Nick hesitated. He didn't mean to—Reese wasn't fishing—but it took him a second to think up an answer that wasn't an actual lie, and that second was all Reese needed.

"Ah," Reese said. "Russell's date went home alone."

Again, Nick wasn't nearly quick enough. Or maybe a flicker of guilt gave him away.

Reese burst out laughing. "Whoa, no, his date did not go home alone. Was it a trade-up? Or did you take double-dating to a whole new level?"

"Noah? Where's your knapsack?"

"What?" Noah looked from Nick to Reese as Reese sputtered with laughter. "What do you mean, take double-dating…" His eyes widened. "No… You mean…?"

"I *mean* get your knapsack," Nick said. "Reese needs his sleep. These shifts are making him giggly."

"So you…? Both? How…? I mean, how does that come up? You ask if they're game?"

Nick could ignore the question. But that wasn't his policy with the boys. Ask anything about anything. That was how Antonio raised him. It also meant never ignoring the opportunity to pass along a lesson or advice.

"No," Nick said. "It has to be their idea. Otherwise, there's going to be hurt feelings afterward."

"Uh-huh," Noah said. "So you wait for women to offer you a threesome? Outside of porn flicks, in what world does that actually happen?"

"In Nick's world," Reese said. "Which can bear a marked resemblance to a porn flick. Kind of a James Bond-high-end porn flick crossover. That's Nick's life."

"No kidding," Noah muttered. "I bet if his car broke down, he'd knock on the nearest door and find sex-starved college girls having an orgy."

"Of course not," Reese said. "In the Nick version, it's classy grown women holding a Tupperware party, which turns into an orgy after he arrives."

"Okay, ha-ha," Nick said. "Are you going to school today, Noah?"

Noah found his knapsack. Nick had to remind him to actually put his homework in it, but five minutes later, they were off and Reese was headed to bed.

As they walked out the door, Noah said, "So, um, not that I'm likely to ever need it, but do you have any advice on threesomes? Like what to do, what not to do, how not to piss one of the girls off. Are there guidelines?"

"There are."

"And you'll tell me?"

"Yes," Nick said. "When you're twenty-one."

"What? There's an age restriction?"

"Yes. It's twenty-one. Before that, it would just be awkward and messy. Get in the car."

• • •

AT TWO THAT afternoon, Nick was driving across town. Very slowly, as one usually drove across New York on a weekday. Normally, he'd have called a driver, but the instructions had been clear. Use your own car. Bring no one with you. He hadn't even been given directions until he was on the road.

All very cloak-and-dagger, which would amuse the hell out of Reese after his James Bond joke. The truth was, Nick's life resembled that of the international spy only superficially. Yes, he had no problems with women. Yes, he had money and knew how to dress, what to drive and so on. He could hold his own in a fight or a car chase. But when it came to true espionage, he left that to the experts. Which is exactly what he'd done with the search for Malcolm.

When Elena and Clay learned Malcolm was alive, they'd known exactly where to find him. In Nast Cabal custody, where he'd apparently been for the last decade, serving a prison term as a thug or an assassin—whatever use they had for a psychotic werewolf. With a Cabal, the possibilities were endless. Malcolm was a prize, and they kept him under tightest security. So he should have been there when Elena negotiated for his return. Except he wasn't.

Elena and Clay had seen Malcolm while he was being escorted from his cell...and while the entire Cabal building was in chaos, after the CEO had been murdered. After they parted, Malcolm saw a chance and took it, killing his guards to escape. Of course, given that the Nasts wouldn't be eager to lose him—or risk a major political incident by refusing to release him—it'd been a while before Elena accepted that he'd really escaped.

Finding out Malcolm was alive had been bad enough. Alive, free, and knowing that Clay would come after him? A hundred times worse. It was a challenge Malcolm wouldn't ignore. He'd be biding his time, waiting for them to lower their guard. Then he'd go after someone—Jeremy, Elena, the kids— to preempt Clay's attack.

All this meant they needed to do more than keep their ears to the ground, waiting for him to surface. They needed to pull in whatever resources they could. For Nick, that meant hiring Rhys Smith's team of supernatural mercenaries.

Rhys's team had been on the job for three months. A guy named Ness was in charge of Nick's case. Though Nick had met a couple of the agents actually tracking Malcolm, he'd only communicated with Ness by text and e-mail. Now Ness was in New York and had an update for him. He wanted to meet face-to-face to discuss it.

The directions led to a motel. As he pulled in, he had to text again for "final instructions," which turned out to be a room number. He was told to park in front of the room. He did...eventually. First, he pulled into the restaurant lot next door and left his car between two rigs, while he slipped around and checked behind the motel. There was a man there, not visibly armed, though Nick was sure he had a gun tucked under his jacket. Rhys's agents didn't rely on their powers alone.

Nick got downwind enough to catch the guy's scent. An ID check of sorts. No one he recognized, so he filed the information.

Next he checked the front of the motel. A guy sat in a pickup reading a map. He'd been reading it since Nick drove in. Another operative.

Nick returned to his car and parked in front of the proper room. It wasn't that he didn't trust Rhys. The guy had nothing to gain from screwing over the Pack. Nick was only assessing the situation before he stepped through that door.

Three

NICK

WHEN NICK KNOCKED, a man opened the motel room door. Mid-forties. Trim. Well-dressed. This, Nick presumed, was Ness, though he didn't ask for an introduction when none was offered. The man escorted him in. Nick noticed a second possibility—a fifty-something guy with a slight paunch. Ness was management level, not a field agent, so the extra weight wouldn't be an issue.

There was also a third person in the room. A woman. All Nick could see of her was her ass. He wasn't complaining, though. It was a very nice ass, a perfectly-rounded curve under a pencil skirt as she bent over a table, writing. There were legs, too, even if they weren't the first thing he noticed. Black nylons with seams running down shapely calves. Black heels, high enough to be sexy, but not impractically so. And there was hair, dark curling waves tumbling almost to the desk as she wrote.

The first man cleared his throat. Nick thought he'd been caught ogling, but the guy only seemed to be getting his colleague's attention. The woman finished what she was doing, straightened and turned, and the view didn't get any worse. She wasn't young—maybe late thirties, and not classically beautiful, but it would have been almost a disappointment if she'd been twenty and gorgeous. This was far more interesting—a striking mature woman with the body of a Forties pinup.

She extended a hand and walked over. "Vanessa."

It took a moment for him to make the connection. He'd been so certain of his contact's gender, and he mentally kicked himself for his presumption.

"Ness?" he said.

She smiled. "Yes, but it's only my code name. In person, it's Vanessa, please."

They shook hands.

"Normally these guys would give you a pat-down, but considering what you are, you don't need a weapon to kill me. So I think we can skip that part."

She dismissed the two men, and they left to stand guard outside. Vanessa waved Nick to a table with two chairs. He took one. As he sat, she flipped through a sheaf of pages.

"I'm sorry to call you away on such short notice," she said. "But I was in town on business, and there's been a break in your case. It seemed like a good opportunity for us to meet, rather than send another agent to update you."

"Thank you."

"You have been pleased with the agents I sent to update you, though, haven't you?"

She continued flipping pages, gaze down, but there was a note in her voice that made Nick tense.

"I know they were pleased with you," she said before he could answer. "*Very* pleased."

Now Nick intentionally didn't reply, waiting and gauging her voice, her posture.

Vanessa lowered herself into the remaining chair. "I'm wondering if there's a specific type you'd like me to send next time, Mr. Sorrentino. Blonde? Redhead? Brunette?"

Shit.

She continued. "I debrief my agents after they meet a client. They don't hold anything back. Whatever happened on a mission—or in a meeting—I hear about it."

Nick straightened. "I don't know what Jayne told you, but I can assure you, I did not take advantage—"

"Oh, I know. It was mutual. There's no question of that. I'm just curious how I could send you two of my best, most *professional* agents, and you manage to have sex with both."

"I didn't have sex with Tina."

"No?"

He tried not to squirm. "Technically, no. There was...intimacy. But she offered."

Vanessa stared at him. "During a client information meeting? How does that work? She updates you on the case, then offers you a blow job?"

"There were a few steps in between."

"I should hope so."

The words sounded shocked, but her dark eyes glittered with barely contained laughter, leaving Nick feeling like a cheerleader who's been caught screwing half the football team.

Nick cleared his throat. "If there was a complaint—"

"Far from it. Both agents are eager—very eager—to work with you again."

"Then if I've broken some code of client conduct—"

"If you have, it wasn't one you were informed of. There's no issue with your behavior, Mr. Sorrentino."

He met her gaze. "Then why are we having this conversation?"

She blinked. Silence fell, and now she was the one who looked uncomfortable, as if she'd been called out for gossiping about the cheerleader.

Nick continued. "If there is a problem with my behavior, I apologize. Either way, it will not happen again. Can we move onto my case?"

Another moment of silence. What did she expect? He was sure she found this all very amusing, but it wasn't as if he was some lecher chasing her young and impressionable agents. Jayne and Tina were both very capable women on the far side of thirty. Women who knew what they wanted and weren't afraid to go for it. What they'd wanted was him. With Jayne he'd been game. With Tina, her "offering" had been step one in her seduction plan and ultimately he'd chosen not to go any further.

While Nick was accustomed to teasing in the Pack, this wasn't good-natured ribbing about his sexual escapades from friends. It was mockery from a virtual stranger. His initial flare of interest froze solid, and some of that chill crept into his voice as he said, "May we proceed? I have a five o'clock meeting."

Vanessa updated him on his case, the same sort of thing Jayne and Tina had done. With the agents, it'd been very casual. He'd certainly suggested a formal discussion in a formal atmosphere. But he'd also offered to talk over drinks, never being one to stand on ceremony, and that's what they'd both elected to do. A quiet upscale bar, a few drinks, small talk mingled with business...a relaxed atmosphere that eventually led to Jayne's room...and to Tina's hands under the table, followed by Tina herself.

Nick kept this meeting coolly professional, and Vanessa followed suit. She told him what they'd been doing, and he asked questions. All business.

"The main reason I called you here is to tell you we're following up on a rumor that Malcolm was spotted in Detroit," Vanessa said. "We heard he'd made contact with a half-demon there, someone he'd worked with at the Nast Cabal."

"And the reliability of this rumor, on a scale of one to ten?"

"Eight."

Until now, Nick had been listening, but only half processing. The update had seemed like mere customer service, making sure the client knows you're using his money well. There had been countless rumors over the last few months. Yet Vanessa had never deemed one worth more than a four.

"All right then," Nick said, pushing his chair back. "Give me the details on this half-demon. Name. Bio. Address. I can be in Detroit tonight."

"There's no need for that. I've sent Tina. Once she has visual confirmation of Malcolm Danvers, she'll report back."

"That's not what we agreed on. I said—"

"Yes, I know what you said, and I was told not to argue the point. I did not, however, agree to it. You hired us to find Malcolm Danvers. Once we have accomplished that, unequivocally, he's all yours. But it's our job to confirm it."

"And as the client, I'm relieving you of that responsibility. I have the right—"

"No, I'm afraid you don't, Mr. Sorrentino. The contract states that we will provide confirmation."

Nick knew that. Before signing it, he'd said that proof wasn't required—he only wanted a solid lead. "Ness" hadn't argued in their e-mail exchanges, which he'd interpreted as informal agreement.

Nick folded his hands on the table. "I am asking you to reconsider. I would insist, but I would prefer to ask. I'm sure Tina's a good agent, but Malcolm is unlike anyone she's ever met."

"Tina has tracked a werewolf. Successfully. On a mission in Germany. That's why she's on this case. She's well prepared."

"For a *werewolf*. Not for Malcolm. He'll be onto her before she gets visual confirmation. He was the best fighter in the North American Pack—"

"*Was*. Past tense. Very past. The man is eighty-five, Mr. Sorrentino. Yes, I know werewolves age slowly, but he's an old man."

"No, he's not. The Nasts were experimenting with cryogenic freezing. Elena says he doesn't look much older than

Jeremy. So shave ten years for that. Shave another twenty off for a werewolf's delayed aging."

She leaned back, and he could tell she was mentally calling bullshit on the cryogenics. Just as Rhys had. The Nasts were denying it, and even among supernaturals, cryogenics was a little too Star Wars. They didn't doubt Malcolm looked decades younger than he was. They didn't doubt he acted it, too, or the Nasts wouldn't have been sending him on missions. But a serious threat to a trained operative? No.

"I said Malcolm was the best fighter in his time," Nick continued. "These days that title goes to Clayton Danvers. Who faced Malcolm nine months ago. Clay will be the first to say it was a real fight. A true challenge."

"Because Clayton had just finished dispatching a dozen Cabal security officers. And the only person Malcolm had fought was Elena, who had bested him before Clayton arrived." Vanessa picked up her file and pretended to leaf through it. "I'm sure that's the story you provided in our intake session. Elena turned Malcolm over to Clayton. They faced off. Clayton won, but he was interrupted by the arrival of the guards. That's why you hired us. Not because Clayton couldn't kill him, but because he missed his chance."

"That doesn't change the fact that two werewolves fought Malcolm and both agree he's not a doddering old man—"

"We don't expect him to be. But you hired us for a job, Mr. Sorrentino. I'm going to ask you to let us finish it."

"If Tina goes after Malcolm, he will see her coming. If he sees her coming, he will kill her."

"I disagree."

"And you're willing to stake your agent's life on it?"

"She's not going to confront him. We've established a fifty-yard guideline. Once she receives visual confirmation and provides photographic evidence, Malcolm Danvers is yours. Until then, we have a contract to complete."

● ● ●

NICK CALLED ELENA on his speakerphone. She was in her own car, on her way to get the twins from school.

He filled her in.

"I could go over her head," he said when he finished. "But I'm not sure Rhys would do anything about it."

"He won't," she said. "If she's blocking you, it's on his orders. Although Rhys might think he's above stereotyping werewolves, he can't quite shake the core assumptions. We may not be dumb brutes, but we have a little too much confidence in our ability to kick the ass of any other supernatural. We're an insular group, distrustful of others, and while we've asked for help in this, it's difficult to do so and we're going to wrest back control the moment we can." She paused and he heard her turn signal click as she took a corner. "All of which isn't exactly untrue. But in this case, we're not exaggerating the danger and we're not jumping in too soon. But we can't convince him of that."

"So, your advice...?"

"If they want to take the risk, we can't stop them. We'll both feel sick if anything happens, but we have to trust that they know what they're doing. They could even be right. Malcolm is the Pack's bogeyman. Maybe we've built him up more than he deserves. You warned them. Now we hang tight and pray they don't screw this up and lose him."

A pause. An uncomfortable one, tension zinging along the line, as Nick pictured Elena fighting the impulse to add "Are you okay with that?" She was Alpha, and that meant no waffling, no democratic problem-solving. Her word was law. Which was fine with Nick. Elena struggled with it.

"Works for me," he said, answering the question she couldn't ask. He swore he heard a soft sigh of relief.

"So, otherwise, what's up there?" he asked, and they spent the rest of their mutual drives talking.

Four

VANESSA

VANESSA CALLAS HAD a routine. When the workday was done, she'd mix a gimlet, draw a steaming hot bath, light a candle and settle in with a book. Tonight, it was past nine and she was still sitting in her hotel room, cell phone by her elbow, trying not to gaze longingly at her novel and the hotel bar menu. The candle she'd brought sat on the table. She put her finger to the wick, lighting it, then snuffed it out. Lighting. Snuffing. Waiting.

She was waiting for two calls. One anticipated; one dreaded. The anticipated one was from Tina. After Nick Sorrentino left, she'd phoned and told Tina to take the night off. She was sending in Jayne tomorrow, and the two could tag-team confirmation on Malcolm Danvers. Tina hadn't been pleased, but she'd promised to call once she was checked into her hotel. That was an hour ago.

The dreaded one was from Rhys. She hadn't contacted him, but she was sure Nick had, probably the moment he got out the door. He would complain, and the boss would be pissed. Not because Rhys would want her to hand the case over to Nick. He was the one who'd forbidden it.

"If it was Elena or Clayton, sure," he'd said. "I'd pass it off. They're used to handling situations like this. But Nick? He's used to *helping* them handle situations like this. Outside the Pack, Nick is known as Clayton Danvers' friend or Antonio Sorrentino's son. He has no reputation himself. He's an omega wolf."

The man Vanessa had been working with remotely had not seemed like an omega wolf. The man she'd met this afternoon absolutely did not seem like one. He'd taken charge just fine. But taking charge in a meeting and taking charge in the field were two different things.

"Bottom line," Rhys had said. "We take the risks here, no matter how much he argues. He's not only a Pack wolf. He's the Alpha's BFF, and if we get him killed, it's a shit-storm of trouble for us."

So Rhys wouldn't call to give her crap for refusing Nick's demand. He'd call because Vanessa hadn't done her job. She hadn't kept the client happy. And in this case, she'd had every intention of keeping Nick happy…and the memory of that, and the colossal fuck-up that ensued was why she really needed that gimlet. Maybe two.

Vanessa Callas did not take unnecessary risks. Not in her job. Not in her life. She was smart and she was careful, so smart and so careful that when she did decide to take a chance and do something crazy, she had no idea *how*, and usually ended up making a complete fool of herself. Like she'd done today.

Vanessa was in charge of five agents. Four of them were women, not because Rhys hired her to play den mother, but because after a few months on the job, female operatives usually requested her as their handler. She'd found the balance between boss and bossy older sister, and her agents took comfort in that. It was a closely-knit team, and overnight meetings often resembled sleepaway camp. Which is where Jayne, after a few glasses of wine, started gushing about Nick Sorrentino. Tina pounced on the next Nick update and got her chance, and then she was the one gushing, though it appeared she hadn't been quite as successful as she'd let on.

Nick Sorrentino. The perfect one-night stand. A werewolf with a model-perfect face and athlete-perfect body. Young enough to have the energy for an all-nighter; old enough to realize he wasn't the only one who should enjoy that all-nighter.

Experienced and attentive. And a nice guy. That was, for the women, perhaps the most shocking part of the package.

That's when Vanessa made her decision. She was going to get some of that. God knows, she *needed* some of that. She didn't even care to calculate how long it'd been.

Vanessa was thirty-eight. She'd come to work for Rhys seven years ago. Before that, she'd been with the FBI, zooming up the ranks with such single-mindedness that after a while she no longer even cared about the end goal, wasn't even sure what her end goal was, only knew that it was higher than where she'd currently been. Then she met Rhys and realized work could be more interesting and more fulfilling, especially for a half-demon.

She worked her ass off, which hadn't left much time for more than passing relationships. That seemed fine, until she hit thirty-four and the doctor said if she was planning to have children, she was reaching the end-stretch. At first, she'd been furious—who was he to presume she wanted kids? The more she thought about it, though, the more she realized she did want something, not necessarily children but the relationship they sprang from. An intimate bond with a man, as a lover and a companion.

As she was realizing that, someone introduced her to Roger. At twenty-five, she wouldn't have given him a second look. There was a spectrum of elements that she looked for with any potential mate. Looks, yes. Success, yes. But also intelligence, wit and personality. Score on three out of five, and it didn't really matter which three, you had a winner. Roger...Roger was perfectly adequate in all categories, outstanding in none. Vanessa had decided that was good enough. At least it was at thirty-five, when it seemed a woman was still expected to present an appealing package...and then be thrilled if it attracted anyone at all.

Roger was all for it, even if he did wish she'd drop a few pounds. She had—which was a struggle, given her figure—and she hadn't even pointed out the fact that his spare tire was rapidly becoming tractor-sized. Though he had two kids from his previous marriage, he wanted more. She wasn't set on them but wasn't against them either, so she said sure. First they had to move in together. Then, on the moving day, he announced he'd found someone else. A twenty-five-year-old who was, it seemed, in possession of a more reliable set of ovaries.

That was the end of Roger.

She'd tried a few dates since, but quickly realized she was too angry and disillusioned. The problem was, if you aren't dating, you aren't getting sex. In the last few months, she'd twice found herself in hotel bars, seriously considering an invitation from some fellow traveler. Which meant the situation was growing dire—in her line of work, you know better than to ever go back to a stranger's room. What she needed was a hookup that came with a "not a psycho" stamp of approval. What she needed was Nick Sorrentino.

So when Tina got a solid lead on Malcolm Danvers, Vanessa made an overdue business trip to New York and combined it with the chance to deliver this update to Nick herself. She'd bought a new dress—borderline vampy but revealing little more than curves—and tried not to regret those ten pounds she'd gained back post-Roger. She'd left her hair unpinned. She'd taken extra care with her makeup. Then she'd formulated a plan of seduction. Except, well, she had no experience with it. Still, from what Jayne and Tina suggested, Nick didn't need hard-core wooing. Let him know you're interested and, if he felt the same, you were set. She would let him know she was game, that she wasn't a prude and was perfectly fine with casual sex...at least in theory. The easiest way to convey this message was to bring up Jayne and Tina.

There was a moment, when she first saw Nick, that she doubted the wisdom of her plan. It was not because his bio photos didn't do him justice. In person, Nick Sorrentino looked like he'd just stepped off an ad for Armani or Ferrari. Tall and slender, flawless olive skin, dark wavy hair, deep brown eyes...While he was fifty, being a werewolf, he looked a decade younger. Yet Vanessa was sure Nick Sorrentino would still turn heads when he *did* look fifty. And sixty. And probably even seventy.

But it wasn't his looks that made her hesitate. It was him—his manner and his bearing and his demeanor, quiet and professional, polite and thoughtful. She hadn't expected a smarmy playboy, but maybe, yes, a hint of that, an air that said he was a player and proud of it. When she didn't detect any such sign, she realized her plan might be...unwise. But by then, it was too late. She'd played her hand and insulted him and made a fool of herself.

Now she waited for a call from Rhys, telling her their client was not pleased and he wasn't sure what the hell she'd done, but she was off the case.

When the phone rang, she reached over with trepidation, then saw the caller ID. Mayfair Flowers. Tina Mayfair's codename.

"I can't imagine Detroit is such a tourist hotspot that it took you ninety minutes to find a hotel room," Vanessa said on answering.

When silence returned, she continued, "Tell me you're at a hotel..."

"I made visual confirmation," Tina said. "Just as I was about to leave my post, he came out of his contact's house. It was too dark for a distance photo so—"

"Did I tell you not to approach?" Vanessa said. "Did I *order* you to stand down?"

"But he was right there and it was dark enough for me to get closer for a photo."

"So you got it?"

Silence. Then, "It...wasn't as easy as it seemed. I took a photo, but it was still too far. I needed a better one. I've been following him—"

"No!" Vanessa said. "I don't care if he's twenty feet away standing under a streetlight. You back down now. *Now.*"

"I would but..."

Vanessa gripped the phone, heart rate picking up speed. "But what...?"

"I...It's a stupid thing, and I feel like an idiot. Somehow, I lost him. I got myself into this blind alley."

No, you didn't get yourself there. Malcolm Danvers got you there.

"Get out now," Vanessa said. "Whatever it takes. Just—"

A sharp intake of breath. Then a clatter, as if the phone had hit the pavement.

"Mayfair?" Vanessa called. "Mayfair!"

Another clatter. Then a male voice, "Hello?"

"Who is this?"

"Who is *this*? Did you lose your phone?" the man said, his voice soft. "Or did you lose something else? Yes, I believe you did. Such a shame, too. She's not gone, though. Not yet. I could return her. Would you like that?"

Vanessa struggled not to snap a reply. "Yes, I would."

"I thought so."

The line went dead.

• • •

VANESSA HAD TWO choices. Option one was to cover her ass—and her employer's. Save them the humiliation of admitting they'd underestimated Malcolm Danvers. Call in backup, jump on the next plane to Detroit and pray she could get her agent back.

Option two? Well, option two would result in huge personal and professional embarrassment, and quite likely cost Vanessa a job she loved. It also gave Tina the best possible chance at survival.

Vanessa picked up the phone and dialed.

Five

NICK

T WAS ALMOST nine-thirty, which in the Sorrentino household meant dinner hour. They'd never been early diners, but with Reese working nights, they'd shifted the meal even later, so he could eat right before leaving. No one had considered the possibility of separate dining times. In this house dinner was the one time of the day when everyone could be together, if only for an hour or two. Most times, it was two, the huge meal stretching into the night, culminating in the living room with drinks and more conversation.

Antonio was with them. Nick had picked him up at the airport earlier. He didn't need to—Antonio would be the first to say he could grab a cab. But after being away for a week, he'd much rather get a lift and spend the trip catching up with his son. So Nick always made sure he was there, waiting.

They'd grabbed dinner on the way back, and they were halfway through the meal, food spread across the table, everyone eating as if they hadn't had a bite all day. Part of it was the werewolf metabolism and part was just family custom, feasting when they came together at night.

Noah didn't have the same appetite as the rest of them but always stayed until the end, grazing and listening to the conversation. Tonight Reese was doing most of the talking, which was rare, but he had an issue at the plant and was looking for advice.

They were partway through that discussion when Nick's cell phone buzzed. He was about to shut it off—work or friends could wait until after dinner. But then he saw who it was and said, "I need to take this."

● ● ●

NICK TOOK THE phone outside, where Antonio wouldn't overhear his conversation. Vanessa told him what happened—that Tina had apparently been trapped and kidnapped by Malcolm.

"He wants something," she said. "He's holding her hostage until he gets it."

The only thing Malcolm wanted from Tina was amusement. There was no need to talk to Vanessa when Tina could supply any answers he wanted. As for trading her life for his freedom, that was ridiculous. Malcolm would trust no promise to call off the hunt, and he wouldn't think himself in serious danger anyway.

Nick didn't tell Vanessa that. She wouldn't want to believe him—he could hear in her voice how upset she was, though she tried to hide it. He wouldn't take away her hope, no more than he'd say, "I told you so."

While he was sure Malcolm intended to kill Tina, he also knew he'd keep her alive until she'd served her purpose. Nick could get to her first. To his relief, that seemed to be exactly why Vanessa was calling.

"You know him," she said. "You understand how he thinks."

Nick doubted any sane person could understand how Malcolm thought, but the Pack knew better than to underestimate him, and with Malcolm, that was where outsiders failed.

Nick checked his watch. "I might still be able to catch a flight tonight."

"You can. I've booked seats on the last plane to Detroit, leaving just before midnight. I know you need to pack a bag—"

"I have one ready. I'll be there in an hour."

"Good. The ticket will be waiting. I'll meet you at the gate."

"Meet—? You're—?"

"It's my agent. I'm coming along."

"No. That doesn't help, and it only endangers—"

"I'll see you at the gate."

She hung up. Nick hesitated, then glanced at his watch again. No time to call her back and argue. They'd settle this at the gate.

• • •

NICK HAD TAKEN that phone call in private, because Antonio had no idea he was spearheading the campaign to find Malcolm. If he did...well, Nick was a little old for his father to forbid him to do anything, but in this case, Antonio would sure as hell try.

Antonio knew Malcolm was alive. He'd had to be warned. He thought, though, that Elena and Clay were hunting him. Nick would help, of course. Antonio might even be fine with Nick hiring Rhys's team and liaising with them, as long as any involvement stopped short of Nick getting within a hundred miles of Malcolm. Which was why Nick had said nothing, as hard as it was to keep something like that from Antonio.

There was a reason Nick had no reputation in the werewolf world. Because his father had done everything in his power to shield Nick from the fights and challenges that would earn him one. When he was young, he'd even been forbidden to travel without other werewolves, for fear some mutt would decide to see what Antonio Sorrentino's son was made of.

It'd been a serious point of contention and resentment when Nick was young. He could remember begging Clay to set up challenge fights for him, as Clay climbed the ranks himself. A few times Clay did have a challenger to spare, but even then, when Nick won his bout, all he heard about afterward was Clay.

In the werewolf world, if you didn't have a rep, you were invisible. Then Jeremy became Alpha. A werewolf who'd rarely fought a bout, because Clay would quietly intercept all challengers to protect him. In the past, the Alpha had to be the strongest werewolf in the Pack. But times had changed and Jeremy had other qualities that made him the perfect leader for the twenty-first century. With his ascension, the pressure to gain a reputation eased, and Nick had relaxed. His Pack valued him. Any mutt he encountered discovered he was a perfectly fine fighter. And Antonio could rest easy, knowing his son was safe, which was the main thing.

As for why it was so important, Nick understood that, too. The circumstances of Nick's birth, Antonio's guilt… Even if they never spoke of it, Nick knew what had happened and why Antonio had kept him close and safe.

So Nick made his excuses—Pack business, Elena needed him to check something out—and then he took off. He reached the end of the long lane to see someone there, a blond figure leaning against the gate, and for a moment, he saw Clay, half a lifetime ago, staking out the end of the drive, waiting for him.

"You going somewhere, Nicky? Not after that mutt they spotted in the city, I hope."

But it wasn't Clay. It was Reese. Nick pulled over and put down the window. Reese leaned in.

"Where is he?" Reese asked.

"Who?"

"Malcolm." Reese raised a hand against his protest. "Yeah, I've figured it out. You need to work on your stealth skills, Nick. You aren't very good at it."

Nor was he any good at denying it, especially given his pact of honesty with the boys. "He's been spotted in Detroit. I hired Rhys to find him. There's…a bit of a balls-up. I'm going to sort it out. Yes, Elena knows. No, Antonio doesn't. Obviously, I'd prefer to keep it that way."

"Sure."

The agreement came quickly, surprising Nick. Reese shrugged. "I know how he is. And I know you're not heading off to take on Malcolm yourself."

Nick gave a short laugh. "No. I'm not that stupid. Once I've confirmed the situation, I'll bring Clay in."

"Good."

Reese walked around the car and opened the passenger door. Nick caught and held it.

"I'm coming with you," Reese said. "Yes, it's basic recon work. Yes, you can handle it. But you should have backup."

"I do. One of the agents."

"Doesn't count," Reese said. "This is werewolf business."

Nick hesitated. He'd vowed not to be his father. Yes, he'd protect the boys, but he wouldn't coddle them. But as he paused, his gaze went to Reese's hand, still gripping the door. His two maimed fingers. Chopped off by a couple of mutts in Anchorage, a warning telling Reese to get out of their territory, but also simply for sport. Reese hadn't been ready to handle them. He might be now, but he sure as hell wasn't ready for Malcolm.

"Not this time," Nick said. "I need you here."

"Um, no," Reese leaned down, meeting Nick's gaze. "You need me there. Backing you up."

"Not with Malcolm."

"Because he's a badass. And a psychopath. I've heard the stories. Hell, I heard them all the way in Australia, long after he was supposed to be dead. All the more reason for you to have backup."

"Which I will. With Clay, as soon as I've confirmed the situation. I can handle this, Reese."

"I never said you couldn't."

As Nick stared him down, Reese dropped his gaze, grumbling slightly, knowing that if he insisted, he *was* saying Nick couldn't handle it.

"I'll call if I need you," Nick said.

"Bullshit."

Nick met his gaze. "If I say I will, I will. You know that."

Again, Reese grumbled and looked away, but he nodded, saying a "Fine" that insisted it wasn't fine at all, then shut the door and let Nick drive away without him.

Six

NICK

NICK HAD LESS luck persuading Vanessa to stay behind. Admittedly, he didn't try very hard, after telling Reese he'd have an agent backing him up. He'd already strained the truth a little by saying he'd told Elena. He'd texted to say that the handler lost touch with her agent so he was flying out that night. Once he had visual confirmation of Malcolm, he'd call Clay in. All technically true. He'd just left out the part where Vanessa was pretty damned sure her agent had been kidnapped.

So Nick really should have backup. And Vanessa came fully prepared, with a field agent kit. It was hard to turn down that kind of help.

Vanessa had bought them first-class tickets. Probably assumed he wouldn't fly coach. Not necessarily true—he was as flexible in that as in everything else—but yes, given the choice, he'd take the extra leg and elbow room. Their seats were together, which was less comfortable. While she was obviously very concerned about Tina, he couldn't forget that this whole mess might have been avoided if she'd listened to him. Also, while he wasn't one to hold a grudge, her early mockery still stung. If it wouldn't have been rude, he might have switched his seat. As it was, he just worked quietly on his laptop.

Halfway through the short flight, Vanessa cleared her throat and said, "Tell me about Malcolm Danvers."

He glanced over. She had her laptop out, and what looked like Malcolm's dossier right there, and he wanted to say, "Read it," but that was being pissy. Presumably she had. She followed his gaze, though, and guessed what he'd been thinking.

"I have his file from Elena," she said. "His bio, it seems. Heavily redacted."

"I'm sure she didn't remove anything you need to identify him. Or to know what he's capable of."

"No, but it's like reading the arrest file for someone who was never charged with a crime. You don't see that many allegations without some basis for them, but without a charge or a trial, there's nothing in-depth. No motivation. No insight into the man."

"I'm not sure I can provide that either. I knew him for half my life, but we weren't close. Malcolm had his favorites. Thankfully, I wasn't one of them."

"Who was?"

Nick hesitated, but he could think of nothing Elena wouldn't want him discussing. "Antonio—my father—and Clay. Jeremy was...not the kind of son Malcolm wanted. He looked for substitutes. Antonio was a fighter, and that always topped Malcolm's list of requirements. But when Clay came along...?" Nick shrugged. "Antonio isn't...aggressive. There's no edge. No anger. He fights for the physical challenge. Clay has edge. He was bitten as a child. He embraces his wolf side more than any of us. Malcolm was fascinated by him. He didn't understand him, though. Whatever Clay's rep, he's no psycho. If you threaten his family, he won't think twice about killing you. But otherwise? I've never seen him lay a finger on anyone for sport. He wouldn't understand that, any more than a real wolf would. Violence is for problem-solving. Malcolm didn't get that. If Clay wouldn't hunt mutts, Malcolm blamed Jeremy's influence. It didn't matter how much Clay hated Malcolm—and he hated him more than anyone, for how he treated Jeremy—Malcolm never stopped pursuing him."

"As a substitute son? Or...more?"

"Antonio always thought there was more, at least when Malcolm chased *him*. There was no shortage of women in Malcolm's life. But he had only contempt for them, and humans in general. So..." Nick shrugged. "Maybe some confusion there. Looking to make a connection, whatever that connection might be."

"Is Elena in danger then? If Malcolm wanted a woman of his own kind, there is one now. Only one."

"He won't go after her like that. It'd be easier if he would—we could lay a trap for him. She's a woman so she's weak."

"Except she kicked his ass."

Nick smiled at the thought. "True, but Elena belongs to Clay, so she's relatively safe. Same with me."

"Because you're Antonio's son."

He nodded. "Malcolm never pursued me, but he treated me well. For Antonio's sake. I'd say that means he won't come after me, but I'd never make that presumption. It only means I'm unlikely to draw his immediate fire."

"He'll think twice before attacking you."

"No, but he'll think twice before *killing* me. With Malcolm, that's what counts."

● ● ●

"ACCORDING TO THE GPS from Tina's phone, she was somewhere around here when she called. It was shut off after...Nick?"

They'd arrived in Detroit an hour ago, rented a car and drove to this neighborhood. They'd been walking for about ten minutes as Nick followed the trail. He'd move ahead while Vanessa had been talking. Now he lifted a hand, telling her to be quiet as he listened. The night was still and silent. Nick could see signs that it hadn't always been like that. There had been shops, but they were long closed and boarded up. An empty block, inhabited only by homeless people and vermin. Vermin of the animal variety, that is even gangbangers and dealers didn't see any profit in a place without people. Contrary to what the news reports might suggest, the whole city of Detroit wasn't like this, but there were pockets of it. A modern-day ghost town.

Tina should have taken one look around and known she was being led into a trap. But she'd been too cocky. He'd gotten that vibe from her when they met, and it was part of what made him decide they wouldn't spend the night together. Here, she would have looked around and thought this was the perfect place to catch her prey, without ever once realizing Malcolm was thinking the same thing.

"Stay close," Nick said as he set out.

"We should do this methodically," Vanessa whispered as she jogged to catch up. "She said it was a blind alley so if we cover the area strip by strip—"

"No need," he said. "I have her trail."

"Oh. I forgot…I'll cover you."

She had a gun. Nick hadn't asked how she got it through security—it'd been checked with the rest of her kit, that's all he knew. While she'd readily admitted that she hadn't been in the field for a few years, she seemed to know what she was doing, so he left her to it and focused on Tina's trail.

Even without it, he could have guessed where she was heading—he could see two burnt-out streetlights ahead and a dark roadway that seemed to lead to a dead end.

Sure enough, that's where Tina's trail went. Only hers entered the blind alley, though. That gave him pause, but he continued following the trail until—

The scent hit him so hard that he stopped in mid-stride. It was no stronger than Tina's, but it was like cold fingers reaching deep into his brain to pluck out a memory long buried.

"Malcolm," he murmured.

"Are you sure?"

"Yes, I'm sure," he said, with a little more impatience than he intended.

"Sorry. It's been a decade," she said. "It's just that…you expected to smell him here, so—"

"Werewolves don't forget scents they know that well. Even if I did, I can tell he's a werewolf and he's related to Jeremy." Nick walked to the building on the left. "He was on the roof. He jumped her. Then…" He followed Tina's scent back to the road.

"He took her that way." She pointed back the direction they'd come.

Nick shook his head. "I only smell Tina."

"She escaped?"

"No, he let her go."

Vanessa walked back to the road and looked down it. "That's not possible. She would have called as soon as she found a pay phone."

"He didn't release her. He let her run so he could chase."

"Why?"

"Because it's fun," Nick said and set out along the exit trail.

Seven

NICK

MALCOLM HAD LET Tina run because it amused him, but Nick knew it was more than simple sport. It had saved Malcolm the hassle of transporting her out of this neighborhood. It might be empty here, but there was life a few blocks over. Presumably there was no place nearby he'd deemed suitable to hold her. Also, a quick capture lacked challenge.

As a trained agent, Tina wouldn't flee to the authorities. With her ego, she'd be cursing herself for getting jumped. Also, Malcolm wouldn't simply have released her but would have allowed her to "escape," so she'd think she bested him. That would give her the confidence not to run for help. She'd want to repair her failure. To turn the tables and catch him.

More of a stalking game than a chase. All the while, he'd be herding her.

Their trails confirmed Nick's guess. They'd converge and separate, and he could see Malcolm driving her along a preor-dained path, one that funneled Tina where he wanted her to go, giving her few options to divert from the path and driving her back onto it when she did.

Nick kept Vanessa informed as he went, but they didn't talk otherwise. She watched his back in silence as he tracked. He considered changing forms, but the path was clear enough.

Too clear? That was the question.

Did Malcolm lay this trail for someone to follow? No. The only person who *could* follow it was a werewolf, and Malcolm wouldn't expect that one of the Pack had sent Tina after him. Werewolves didn't hire outsiders to do their dirty work. He'd presume Tina was from the Nasts so he wouldn't worry about his scent trail. Still, Nick kept an eye—and an ear—on his surroundings.

Eventually the trail led to an empty building, abandoned so long that it was impossible to tell what it had been. Maybe a small factory or a school—a two-story rectangular box with-out a window intact.

Nick glanced around the neighborhood. Not really a neighborhood so much as a piece of land with buildings on it, some homes, some commercial, some occupied, some not. At this hour, it was silent. He took one last listen and then led Vanessa through a doorway.

• • •

INSIDE, THE ONLY light came from the moon shining through broken windows.

"Can you see?" Nick whispered to Vanessa.

"Not well."

He gave her credit for admitting it. "Stay close. If you can't see me in front of you, let me know. I'd rather not use flashlights if we can help it."

"If I need to, I have this." She lifted her fingers and they started to glow.

He nodded. She'd explained on the drive that she was an Aduro, a mid-level fire demon. As defensive powers went, it was a good one.

"If you need that, use it," he whispered. "Better than tripping in the dark and making noise."

"I know."

There was no annoyance in her voice, but he murmured an apology nonetheless, as she had when she questioned his scent tracking. Neither was accustomed to working with the other. They had to remember that.

Even inside, Nick couldn't tell what purpose the building had once served. Anything that could leave a hint had been stripped. It was all empty rooms. Well, not really empty— there was plenty of junk, but most of it seemed to have been brought in by squatters over the years.

Now, though, he could hear no signs of life. When he passed one room, he caught the scent of a corpse. A recent one. Human. Male. He smelled blood, too, meaning the man hadn't died of a drug overdose or natural causes.

As they passed the room, Vanessa lit up her fingers and waved them inside, illuminating a corpse, sitting up, throat ripped out.

"Werewolf?" she whispered.

Nick didn't answer right away. It was a classic werewolf murder, which made him slow to reply. It's not easy to tear out someone's throat when you're in human form, so there was a moment where he wondered if it really was Malcolm's work. But then he caught the scent and when he moved closer, he found a few dark hairs caught in the man's ripped flesh. Wolf fur. Malcolm had changed form and cleared the building, scaring out those who would run and killing those who wouldn't.

Nick told Vanessa, and she gazed down at the body. Her expression wasn't cold, but it wasn't horrified either. There was disgust there. More consideration, though, before turning to him and saying, "I'm sorry."

"For what?"

She nodded at the body, and then waved around the building, and he knew what she meant. Sorry that she'd thought he was exaggerating. That she'd underestimated Malcolm.

"Let's find Tina," he said.

She nodded and followed him out of the room.

● ● ●

THEY FOUND A second body. A girl. Maybe seventeen. A street kid. She lay on her back, long sleeves ripped as if she'd tried to protect her throat as the wolf leapt on her. That death hit harder, and it took a moment to move on. When they did, Nick heard a sound. The whisper of fabric on concrete, so faint he thought he'd imagined it until he made Vanessa stop moving and caught the noise again. It sounded like something being dragged across the concrete floor.

No, not something—someone.

He followed the sound. They were on the second floor and the noise seemed to come from the middle. When he approached, his arm shot out, stopping Vanessa. He motioned for her to light her fingers and look. She did. There, ahead, part of the floor was missing, and they could see down to the first level. A body lay in the middle of the room.

"Tina," Vanessa whispered.

Nick caught her before she could move closer to the hole. She didn't push him off but leaned and strained to see better.

Tina lay on her stomach. Drag marks led to a blood pool ten feet behind her.

"Is she...?" Vanessa asked.

He was about to say he couldn't tell when Tina moved, one arm slowly reaching out as she propelled herself forward. That was the sound he'd heard, the swish of her clothes as she dragged herself toward the door.

Vanessa exhaled. She started forward, but this time caught herself.

"It's a trap, isn't it?" she whispered.

Nick nodded.

"But we can't leave." She straightened. "I have an agent down. That's my priority, above my own safety."

She looked over, as if expecting him to argue. He didn't. If it was a Pack brother, he'd do the same. He waved her back to the hall, where they could come up with a plan.

Eight

VANESSA

LEAVING TINA WAS one of the hardest things Vanessa had ever done. Even if she knew she wasn't abandoning her, that's what it felt like. Her agent—her friend—was lying in her own blood, badly injured, and she'd walked away.

They came up with a plan as quickly as possible. Then they separated. Vanessa retreated to the stairs, moving as fast as she could. She zipped down them, then slowed, listening for the faintest creak or scuff of a footfall.

How badly had she screwed up here? Worse than she ever had before. It didn't matter if Rhys had refused to let Nick take over. It didn't matter if Vanessa had warned Tina off and called Jayne in to assist. She did not accept excuses from her team and she would not make excuses here. Whatever had happened to Tina—whatever was happening now—it was her fault.

Nick had stayed upstairs to stand watch over Tina and to avoid spreading his scent farther through the building. She had to struggle to factor scent into the equation. It required a bigger mental leap than she would have imagined. A werewolf could track his prey, no matter where she ran. A werewolf could smell someone nearby, even if they were silent and hidden. And a werewolf could recognize another by scent. Thinking that way was as normal for them as using her built-in flashlight was for her.

Rhys had a werewolf on the team, and she'd prided herself in thinking she knew all about them because she'd once spearheaded a huge operation with him. Now she realized that was as ridiculous as saying you understand another culture because you have one friend from it.

As she continued across the first floor, she didn't detect anyone else around. She gripped her gun, the fingers on her free hand lit, not just for light, but to jumpstart her powers if Malcolm leaped at her from the shadows. That's what he seemed to have done to Tina. Werewolves didn't use guns—even the one on Rhys's team balked at it. From the Nast file, Malcolm had refused to use anything but his fists. They'd send him out with a gun or blade, only to find he'd left it behind, as if even carrying it spoke of weakness.

So Vanessa kept moving, as quickly as she dared, poised for attack. As she turned a corner, she heard a scratching sound. She wheeled, her back to the wall, gun ready. The sound came again, from the direction they'd left Tina. Was it Tina herself? God she hoped so. With every step of the seemingly endless walk downstairs, she'd thought of Tina breathing her last, alone, as Vanessa crept toward her.

She continued, inching along the wall now, struggling to check her speed. The sound grew louder, and Vanessa knew she was close. She moved to the open doorway and stopped.

There was Tina, sprawled on the floor, a few feet farther from that puddle of blood. One arm was outstretched to drag herself along, but only her fingers moved, scratching the concrete floor as if her strength was gone and she was too far into shock to realize the futility of it. Vanessa gripped the wooden doorjamb so hard she smelled smoke. She only gripped harder, struggling not to race into the room.

That's what he wants. You see her there, dying, and run to her.

Now came the time for trust. To trust that a man she barely knew would watch her back.

She couldn't look up to confirm Nick was there, watching through the hole. If Malcolm was nearby, he'd notice. She walked forward with her gun out, fingers blazing, knowing that was still not enough to save her from Malcolm. Only Nick could do that. She had to walk into the middle of that floor, an open target.

"Tina?" she whispered.

Tina kept scratching at the floor.

What if this was the trap? What if he'd promised Tina freedom in return for luring in her employers? From here, the only sign of injury was the blood, which wasn't necessarily even hers.

Vanessa would like to say Tina wouldn't do that, but of all her agents, Tina was the least reliable, as proven by her refusal to stand down tonight.

Vanessa should have thought of this. Warned Nick. But it was too late. If this was the trap, she had to be ready.

Vanessa moved to Tina's side and lowered herself to one knee. She could hear Tina's breathing, shallow and labored. When she touched the woman's shoulder, Tina didn't tense, didn't react at all, just kept scratching the floor.

She gripped Tina's shoulders with both hands, her fire extinguished, her gun on the floor, intentionally leaving herself vulnerable. Tina still didn't respond. Vanessa carefully turned her over and—

She sucked in a breath. Tina's throat was…Vanessa had seen Malcolm's other two victims, their throats savaged, a bloody mess of tissue and gore. He hadn't done that to

Tina. He'd slit her throat just enough to let her bleed out. Slowly.

Vanessa's burning fingertips flew to Tina's neck, pulling the flesh together, then cauterizing the wound to stop the bleeding. Field medicine—a skill she'd learned from another fire half-demon on Rhys's team.

She closed the wound, her fingers trembling. And then… And then she looked at Tina and knew it was too late. The wound hadn't been doing more than seeping blood. The critical loss was back there, a dozen feet away. Tina still breathed, heart pumping, but her eyes were empty, her hand flexing, as if she was still scratching at that floor, the instinct for survival outlasting all other mental functions.

Vanessa told herself she was wrong. Had to be wrong. Tina was alive. Just in shock. The wound was cauterized and now they just needed to get her to help.

She whipped around, looking for Nick, annoyed that he wasn't already here to help. When she caught a flicker of motion, she remembered why he wasn't and grabbed for her gun, but it was only Nick, leaping from the second floor as easily as if it'd been a two-foot hop.

"We need to get her help. There's a clinic—"

"She's gone, Vanessa," he said softly.

"No, she's breathing. She's alive. She can get a transfusion. Help me lift—"

"Vanessa?" He took her shoulder and before she could throw him off, he turned her to look down at Tina, lying unmoving on the floor.

"No," she whispered. She dropped to her knees and looked into Tina's eyes, wide and staring blankly. Then she heard a rattle, deep in the woman's chest.

"She's alive. She..."

Tina's lips parted, and she exhaled. Then she went still.

Vanessa's hands slammed down on Tina's chest, pumping, starting CPR. She knew it was useless. She'd known she couldn't save Tina from the moment she saw that hole in her throat and that look in her eyes. Tina had been lost before they even made it to the building, staying alive by sheer will, too far gone to revive.

That didn't stop Vanessa from performing CPR, even as she swore she could feel Tina's body cooling. At last, she felt Nick's hand on her shoulder, fingers resting there, telling her what she already knew—they had to go.

Vanessa pulled back and stared down at Tina. The hole in her throat was almost medically precise in its placement. No knife had made it, though. The edges were jagged, as if Malcolm had...she wasn't even sure how you'd do that. Bite? Rip? Whatever he'd done, there was no way Tina sat still and took it. Yet it would be impossible to be that precise with a struggling—

She bent and ran her hands over Tina's head. There it was. A goose-egg, also expertly placed. He'd brought her here, questioned her, knocked her out and then cut her throat. That's why there'd been one blood pool. Tina had almost bled out, then somehow regained consciousness and crawled away.

Vanessa rose. Nick had moved off now, scouting the area and occasionally dropping into a crouch, presumably sniffing.

"It was definitely Malcolm," he said, though she knew he was checking for her benefit only. He knew who this was. No one else would be this sadistic.

"It wasn't a trap for us, was it?" she said. "He didn't even stick around to watch her die."

"It would seem not," he said slowly, looking around, frowning.

"You don't detect any sign of him, do you?"

"No, it's just...It seems odd."

"Only if you presume he knew someone would come after Tina tonight, which would have been nearly impossible if we weren't relatively close already." She reached down to touch the pool of blood. It was already tacky. "It's been at least an hour. Maybe two."

"And he tired of waiting, I suppose. I'll hide her body for now. You have someone who can come to retrieve it?"

"First thing in the morning. For now, I need to notify Rhys."

Vanessa retreated to a corner to do that. She kept her back to Tina's body. It was the only way she could focus. Seven years on the job and she'd never lost an agent. She'd been so proud of her record, and now she realized it'd been dumb luck. No matter how many precautions you took, it was never enough. There was always something to miss, blame to take—

She pushed off the thought and made the call.

Nine

NICK

NICK CIRCLED THE room as Vanessa made her call. There was no reason to give Tina that slow death if no one would witness it. Had Malcolm known her backup was coming? She must have talked enough to let him know she was an operative. Having been one himself, he'd know that the phone call he'd interrupted would have triggered backup, possibly even from someone already in the city.

So why wasn't Malcolm here? Nick was quite certain he'd left—the trail he found was cold, and when he followed it as far as he dared, it continued on toward the back of the building. There was no trace of Malcolm's scent in the surrounding rooms to suggest he'd lain in wait. Nor had there been any on the upper level, near the hole.

This was, admittedly, the point where he'd normally turn to Elena or Clay and say, "What do you make of this?" That would be the extent of his responsibility—noting something out of place. Hell, most times they'd be two steps ahead of him already.

He circled the room one last time. Then he stopped short.

"We need to go," he said, turning to Vanessa.

She was still on the phone and raised a finger, telling him to hold on.

He strode over. "No, we need to leave. It's a trap. We're in a building with at least three dead bodies and—"

As if on cue, he picked up the distant creak of a floorboard.

"*Now*," he said.

She signed off. "We need to move Tina—"

"Too late. Someone's coming."

"We should wait," she said. "Hide and see what's going on."

"I know. But not here. Come on."

● ● ●

NICK AND VANESSA watched as three people stood around Tina's body. Three men dressed in dark clothing, two holding guns, the third a knife. Big guns—.45 caliber, he'd guess. The knife wasn't small either, and from the bulge under the guy's jacket, he had a gun there too.

They weren't werewolves. Nick could tell that from his hiding spot, their scent drifting far enough to pick up. They looked like...Well, that was the thing. To the untrained eye, they looked like commandos or mercenaries, like guys who'd work for someone like Rhys. Except, having met people who worked for Rhys, Nick knew that real mercenaries sure as hell didn't advertise their occupation with their outfits and equipment. They dressed and acted like ordinary people. Blending in. Invisible.

These guys looked like they were in the middle of a role-playing game. Pretending to be mercenaries. They were physically suited to the role, at least the stereotype of it. All three were younger than forty. None under six feet. All square-jawed and bristle-haired. It'd be an amusing spectacle, actually, if they weren't standing over the corpse of a woman he'd known.

It'd also be more amusing if those guns weren't so damned big.

One dropped to his knee beside Tina.

"Looks different than the others," one of his companions said.

"Different but the same. Still a werewolf kill. Seems as if he got interrupted here. Started tearing out her throat and something stopped him."

"Think he heard us coming?"

The kneeling guy, who seemed to be the leader, touched the blood trail. "Nah. It's dry."

"She's different, too." That was the third guy, his hair so short he might have been bald. "Definitely no hobo. Are we sure it's our target's handiwork?"

"No," the leader said. "It's some random dude who just happened to slit her throat in the same building that two people had their throats ripped out by our target. Of course it's him. Weres have two kinds of victims—those who won't be missed and pretty women."

He was actually right. For man-eaters at least, those were their favored victims. The disenfranchised satisfied the urge to hunt and kill with little fear of the authorities noticing. Women satisfied another kind of hunting urge. If that was the case, though, there'd be signs that Tina had been raped or, at least, had sex recently. They didn't check for that. Nick suspected they didn't care. They knew the type of prey their target favored, and that was enough.

The leader rose. "Okay, let's fan out. See if this bastard left any clues."

• • •

THIS WAS, ONE could argue, the point at which Nick should get the hell out of Dodge. He was a werewolf, and these guys were looking for a werewolf. Bounty hunters of some type, he guessed, on Malcolm's trail. *That* was the trap. Let Tina die slowly, knowing these guys were coming. Either they'd find her alive and slow down to help her—or, if her handler had dispatched backup, the arrival of three armed bounty hunters would throw a wrench into the works. Either way, it let Malcolm slip off scot-free.

So Nick should go after Malcolm. And he did. He followed the trail out of the building, over two blocks, where it disappeared at the roadside, meaning Malcolm had hopped into a car and escaped. There was no tracking him after that.

"I want to know who those guys are," he said to Vanessa as they walked. "If they've separated, I can grab one. Question him."

"That's what I'd suggest," she said. "Except for the part where *you* question him. We don't want him seeing you."

"We'll work something out."

● ● ●

As THE LEADER said, the men had split up. Vanessa left Nick in charge of tracking. He knew which one he wanted. The nearly-bald guy. More brawn than brains. He'd fight the most, but he'd break first, too. That's what Clay always said, which is why, in a fight, he often left the biggest guy to Nick.

Now he was tracking his target, with Vanessa as backup. It didn't take long before he could hear the guy, who made no effort to hide his footfalls. Nick veered left, taking Vanessa down another hall. Soon she could hear the guy too, in the parallel hall. They continued on to the next adjoining corridor. Nick turned to intercept and Vanessa carried on.

Nick came out behind the guy. He moved cautiously, rolling his footfalls, and Nick closed the gap until he was a few feet behind his target. Then he slowed and listened. After a moment, he heard Vanessa's footsteps. The guy heard them, too, a few seconds later.

The guy stopped. Nick halted behind him, barely breathing. The target raised his gun and dropped his free hand to his side, brushing his radio. He must know he should notify his team, but he couldn't bring himself to call in backup. He straightened and strode forward.

Vanessa turned the corner. She seemed to see their target at the last second and wheeled, her eyes going wide. Vanessa wasn't what the man expected, and he stopped short.

That's when Nick lunged. His pounce was silent, he was sure of that. But the guy must have sensed something behind him. He spun, gun rising. Nick slammed a backfist into the side of his head. The guy flew off his feet and hit the ground.

"Nice," Vanessa murmured as she knelt, confirming the man was out cold.

He let Vanessa bind the man's hands with plastic cuffs, blindfold and gag him, then Nick loaded the limp body over his shoulder and carried him out of the building.

Ten

NICK

BEFORE THEY HAD returned to take a hostage, Nick had detoured to a building next door. It was much smaller, but equally empty. Perfect for an interrogation. Now Vanessa stood watch as he carried the man across the gap. Halfway there the guy began stirring. Nick picked up his pace. By the time he was inside, the man was kicking and grunting against his gag. Nick got him into the first room and dumped him on the filthy floor.

Vanessa warned the man that she was going to remove his gag, and there was no sense calling for help—lying that they'd driven him far from his companions. The moment the gag came off, though, he started to yell. He got one note out before Vanessa pistol-whipped him in the exact spot where Nick had punched him. Even Nick winced. The man started to yowl, but Nick was already yanking the gag back into place.

Vanessa repeated the warning. This time, he seemed to decide he ought to listen. Also, he now realized Vanessa wasn't alone.

"Who's your partner?" he said, whipping his head about, as if he could peer through the blindfold.

"An associate."

"I saw him inside. I've seen him before, too."

Nick tensed.

"And where have you seen him?" she asked.

"I...I dunno. But I got a look at him right before he decked me."

"Describe him, then."

The guy stammered and blustered, saying Nick had dark hair and he was "huge, bigger than me." Nick had to smile at the second part. Obviously that line-drive to the head had colored the man's recollection of his size. It also seemed to have scrambled any memory of what he actually had seen, which couldn't have been more than a fleeting glimpse.

Vanessa quickly moved on to the interrogation. Nick let her handle it.

Nick had some knowledge of interrogation techniques. Well, the kind Clay used, at least, which usually involved his fists. Clay would prefer something more intellectual—the guy was a PhD, after all—but as he'd said many times, that wasn't the language mutts spoke. You had to beat answers out of them.

It was different with this guy. Or it was, following a second pistol-blow to the same spot. After that, Vanessa eased into a completely different form of questioning. The kind where she claimed she was only doing her job, regretted it even, and sounded as if she genuinely did.

"Look, I overheard you guys in there," she said. "You're hunting a werewolf. I have no issue with that. Filthy, murdering scum. Did you see what they did to my colleague?"

It took a moment for him to realize she meant Tina. "She was with you?"

"Yes. I have a feeling you and I are after the same guy. But you aren't authorized to take him out. I checked with my superiors. There's no record of an alternate license being issued."

"License…?"

"For hunting him."

Silence as the guy's brain whirred. "Since when do we need a license to hunt vermin?"

"Since when *don't* you? The Cabals regulate the hunting of all werewolves and vampires. You do know that, right? And if you pretend you don't know what a Cabal is…"

"Of course I do. But I don't know nothing about them regulating hunting."

"Then I'd suggest you look into it, because if you're caught? The penalty is stiff, as you might imagine."

He paled, likely imagining a fate worse than any Cabal would actually impose…if they did regulate "hunting."

Nick mouthed a question to Vanessa, who nodded.

"So that's what you're doing then," she said. "Hunting vermin? Or is it a bounty?"

"Both."

"Hunting *vermin* for a bounty? On just this particular werewolf?"

The man shrugged. "Nah, any werewolf would do. The guy just wants them exterminated, and he's willing to pay to see it happen. Win-win."

"Exterminated?" Vanessa said.

"Well, controlled. You can't just wipe them out, right? Not that I'd argue if you could. World would be a better place without those brutes."

Nick stiffened. This was something he would never get used to. When he'd grown up, the Pack had kept itself separate from the greater supernatural world, and he'd never had cause to wonder what others thought of them, because as far as he knew, no one believed in them.

Then the Pack rejoined the interracial council, and he'd found out exactly what they thought of him. Namely that he was a brutish killing machine, liable to rip their throats out for kicks.

"So someone's putting out bounties on werewolves," Vanessa said. "Besides general cleanup, what's his motivation?"

The guy was still blindfolded, so they couldn't see his eyes, but his face screwed up in confusion. "Motivation?"

"Did this guy lose someone to a werewolf?"

"Not that I know of. He just doesn't like them. He considers it his...what's it called? Civic duty. As a supernatural."

Nick mouthed another question.

"Let me step back then," Vanessa said. "Do you know who you're hunting?"

"It's not a who. It's a what. They aren't human. You can't think of them that way."

Nick rocked on the balls of his feet.

"Let's pretend it's a who," Vanessa said. "For simplicity's sake, since you already know *what* it is. Do you know the identity of the one you're hunting now?"

A pause. A long one. Then, "Pete does."

"Pete?"

"The team captain. He gets all that intel. We're not supposed to ask."

"Okay, so Pete knows who he's tracking. How was he tipped off?"

Another pause. "Pete handles all that."

"And do you know anything about it? When he found out? Who told him?"

More silence. Then, defensively, "That's not how it works. The team doesn't get details."

Vanessa prodded some more, but after that it was obvious that whatever more he knew wasn't worth prying out of him. The facts seemed clear enough. Someone was putting out bounties on werewolves and had set these guys on Malcolm's tail. Then Malcolm discovered he had two groups to contend with—the bounty hunters and Rhys's mercenaries—and used one to distract the other while he fled.

When they were certain they could get no more from their captive, Vanessa refastened his cuffs with another, looser pair that he'd be able to wriggle out of…after they were long gone.

Eleven

VANESSA

INA WAS DEAD. Murdered horribly. Vanessa kept thinking "What if we'd been a few minutes quicker? What if we hadn't been so careful?" It wouldn't have made a difference. She knew that. Yet logic didn't help, because she'd seen Tina alive, seen her moving, and there was part of her that insisted her operative could have been saved. That she'd failed.

Dwelling on that was self-indulgent, though. There was a job to do—stopping Tina's killer. Grief would come later.

It wasn't just Malcolm they needed to worry about now. She was with a werewolf and there were three idiots in town on a werewolf hunt.

Vanessa could tell that conversation had upset Nick. No one wants to think another person would hunt them down as "vermin." But she hadn't expected him to seem quite so shocked. Because she wasn't. That's when she realized that no matter how liberal she considered her own views she still, in a way, supported the stereotypes by not being shocked, not being outraged.

As they walked out of the building, she wanted to tell him she'd never heard of such bounties, that these men were clearly thugs of the lowest order. Except she'd be lying. Not about the thugs part. They obviously were. But supernaturals *did* hunt werewolves and vampires. Not often, and they usually weren't successful. Given that there were only a few dozen of each on the continent, more than the very rare death would be noticed, and the werewolves and vampires would retaliate.

They *should* retaliate and put an end to it. It wasn't as if the hunters would fight back. They were like humans going after big game. They knew if their prey got within ten feet of them, they'd be dead. So why didn't werewolves and vampires put a scare into hunters? Because they didn't know about them. Because people like the Cabals and Rhys's teams didn't bother to warn them. Didn't want to stir them up because that was just inconvenient.

As they neared their rented car, Vanessa said, "It does happen."

Nick looked over, his dark brows gathering.

"Hunting werewolves. And vampires. I've heard of it."

She braced for him to stiffen. To ask why they didn't tell the Pack. But he only nodded.

"I've heard of it, too," he said. "But not in North America. It's a big problem in areas without a Pack, and there are plenty of those. Supernaturals go there to hunt. Elena even found an encrypted website offering tours." His lip curled. "Come and hunt the werewolves. We'd never heard of it here, though. I'll have to let Elena know."

And that was it. No blame. No accusation. He didn't complain because it was exactly what he'd come to expect. This was how werewolves were treated.

"You should have been told," Vanessa said. "Your Pack, that is."

Nick shrugged and opened the rental car door. "We'll handle it."

They got into the car.

"It shouldn't happen in the first place," she said. "They're red-neck idiots. If they were human, they'd be out hunting illegal immigrants or small-time crooks. They just need an excuse."

"Oh, I know. It's not like werewolves have never done that themselves." He started the car. "Historically, we hunted mutts—outside werewolves. They'd say it was to keep them in line, but really, they were like these guys. They wanted to hunt, so they came up with an excuse."

Nick drove out of the parking spot. "We have a Pack member now whose dad was killed in a mutt hunt when he was fifteen. They knew his father had a kid. Didn't care. They wanted to kill him, too. He's lucky he escaped." He glanced over. "Want to guess who was in charge of that hunt?"

"Malcolm."

"Yep. So that's another Pack wolf we aren't telling about his return. Too many folks lined up to kill the bastard already." He reached the road and turned left. "Speaking of Malcolm, that's my target here. If Elena wants to come out and handle these losers, fine, but I'm guessing she'll see it as a wild goose chase. Easier to get to the root of it and work from there."

"Find out who's laying the bounties instead of hunting down three knuckleheads taking them." Vanessa nodded. "She's smart."

"That's why she's Alpha. Give that choice to some of the guys and they'd hunt the bastards down. That's the instinct. But these days? There are other ways. The point, though, is that my goal is Malcolm, and his trail is warm. I'm going to pay a visit to his contact in Detroit. You don't need to come along. It's been a long night and after Tina…" He shrugged. "I can drop you at a hotel and check back with an update in the morning."

"I'll give you the guy's address," she said. "But I should go along, as backup."

He said nothing.

She continued, "I won't interfere. As far as I'm concerned, after what happened to Tina, you're in charge. You're the one who understands what we're dealing with. While I'm not a field agent these days, I can still watch your back and provide whatever other support services you need."

"All right. Pull up the address and tell me where to go."

Twelve

NICK

BEFORE THEY REACHED their destination, Nick pulled over. He had to update Elena, and he wanted to do that in private. Vanessa had her own call to make. She'd texted Rhys an update, but he wanted to speak to her about getting Tina's body back.

Nick had hated leaving Tina behind. At the very least, he'd wanted to hide her body, but the arrival of the hunters quashed that plan.

He left Vanessa in the car so they could make their respective calls.

Elena and Clay hadn't gone to bed after he'd said he was leaving for Detroit. They probably had bags packed, ready to hop in the car for the six-hour drive, but more than that, they just wanted to be on the other end of the line if he needed to talk.

Elena put him on speakerphone. There was no need for subterfuge. Jeremy had taken the twins for a weekend trip to visit Jaime, who was doing a show in Charleston.

"So it's definitely Malcolm," Clay said after Nick explained about finding Tina. "Good."

"What he means," Elena said, "is, 'Damn, it's a shame Malcolm killed that poor woman.'"

Nick chuckled. He knew Clay would no more think about Tina than he'd consider whether a shirt really was the right color for his complexion. It just didn't enter his head.

"Did you know her well?" Elena asked.

"I'd met her. We had drinks. Obviously, it was a bit of a shock, but it's harder on Vanessa. She's holding up well, though, probably because she hasn't had too much time to process it."

He told them about the bounty hunters.

"Son of a bitch," Clay said. "Bounties? Here?"

"Vanessa said it happens."

"And no one bothered to tell us?"

"I'll raise a stink," Elena said. "Let Clay knock some heads together so they get the hint. Mostly, though, we need to make sure these guys don't pick up your trail. They sound more of a nuisance than anything, but they could get in the way. Did they get a look at you?"

He explained.

"So he's probably seen your picture somewhere," Elena said.

Clay grunted. "Hopefully on a list of 'werewolves you do not fuck with or you'll bring the whole Pack down on your head.'"

"Hmm," she said. "Did they seem to *know* you're a werewolf?"

"Definitely not," Nick said. "I'll keep my eyes open, but they're on Malcolm's trail not mine. Which is still inconvenient. Not that I think they stand a hope in hell of taking him down, but there's always dumb luck."

"You want me to hop in the car?" Clay asked.

Nick was about to answer when he realized Clay wasn't asking him.

"It's up to Nick," Elena said. "He's handling it fine, but if he wants to get rid of Vanessa, then we'll go. Rhys will squawk, but he doesn't have much leverage here. He screwed up not letting Nick take over."

"I'll grab our bags," Clay said.

"Hold on," Nick said. "I didn't answer yet."

Clay made a noise, as if to say this was merely a formality. Of course Nick would want him there.

"Let's wait," Nick said. "We've got werewolf hunters in town, and you're the most recognizable werewolf in the country."

"So? They come after me, we end the problem."

"And have three bodies to bury?" Elena said.

"Nah. One, maximum. I'll just scare the shit out of them and make them realize this werewolf-hunting thing isn't as much fun as they thought."

"While Malcolm escapes?"

Silence. Clay sighed. "All right. But our bags are packed. Find Malcolm and give us a call."

"I will."

● ● ●

THEY WERE IN the suburbs, outside a house big enough to hold a family with five kids and two dogs. As Nick surveyed the place from the idling car, he said, "So the guy doesn't live alone."

"Just him and his wife."

He glanced over. "Kids grown?"

Vanessa shook her head. "No kids. He took advantage of a really bad real estate market." She waved down the road. "Half these places are empty. Foreclosures everywhere."

Which explained why the street was so dark. They'd driven through other neighborhoods that seemed to be thriving, but this—like that downtown street of vacancies—was what people thought of when you said "Detroit" these days. Nick looked at the huge house. It'd be less of a bargain when they were paying to keep it heated during a Michigan winter.

"Any idea which houses are empty?" he asked.

After a minute of flurried typing on her phone, Vanessa said, "I can tell you."

"Direct me to one farther down. We'll park there."

Thirteen

NICK

THEY'D PULLED RIGHT into the garage after Nick snapped the lock and yanked the door open. Then they took the back way to the contact's house.

The contact was Richard Stokes. A sorcerer, married to a half-demon named Sharon. According to Vanessa's sources Stokes worked for the Nasts as a hit man, which is how he'd gotten to know Malcolm. They'd done a few jobs together—the Nasts sending them out as tag-team assassins.

From all accounts, Malcolm did not like partners. His first two had suffered unfortunate and fatal accidents during their mission. Malcolm had barely bothered trying to disguise what he'd done. Even his excuses had been perfunctory at best. That was Malcolm flexing his muscles and nudging his boundaries, seeing how badly the Cabal wanted him. His "story" became the official record to avoid executing him, though they punished him for "failing to protect his partner from harm."

With Stokes, they found a partnership model that worked, namely because it wasn't a partnership at all. Stokes wisely did his research on werewolves and figured out that Malcolm shouldn't theoretically have a problem sharing his jobs. Wolves were Pack hunters. The issue was one of hierarchy. Stokes had let Malcolm take the lead, and it turned into a beautiful friendship. Or at least a functional working relationship.

In the Pack, every wolf who ran with Malcolm was never allowed to forget what a privilege that was. They owed him for the benefit of his companionship. In the last decade, though, Malcolm hadn't had his usual pack of sycophants. He'd only had one. Richard Stokes.

When Malcolm escaped then, it wasn't long before he'd showed up on Stokes' doorstep demanding payment in services, information and money. That put Stokes in a very ugly position. If the Nasts found out that he'd had contact with their valuable escapee, they'd kill him. If he ratted out his former partner, Malcolm would kill him. So Stokes had played both sides. He did help Malcolm. Meanwhile, he told the Nasts and got them to agree to let him keep aiding their escapee until Malcolm lowered his guard enough to be safely brought back in. All that information had come through a mole Rhys had in the Nast Cabal.

Now Nick and Vanessa were at the Stokes' back door, under cover of night, evaluating the situation after having donned disposable gloves from Vanessa's kit.

The dark house meant Stokes and his wife had gone to bed. Which made things easier. It did, however, increase the chance they'd startle the two and get hit with a blast of spell and half-demon power.

The first obstacle was a potential security system. Luckily, Vanessa had a device to detect it and the skills to disarm it. When the detection device came back negative, she hesitated.

"That doesn't seem right," she said. "He's a professional killer. He knows the value of security."

Nick shrugged. "Maybe he thinks being a killer means he doesn't need it."

"Hmm."

She picked the lock. It opened easily. In fact, the entire door opened, the deadbolt having been left unfastened. Nick looked at that, then craned his head in the door to see a security alarm, flashing green.

"Bolt not used, alarm turned off. Shit." He stepped into the house and inhaled deeply. "I smell blood."

Vanessa moved past him to survey the dark kitchen. Nick dropped to a crouch and inhaled again.

"Malcolm," he murmured.

"Since we last saw him?"

"I can only judge the relative age of a trail, but it's fresh, meaning it's not from earlier."

"All right then. Let's go see what he's done."

She lifted her gun and started forward. Then she stopped.

"Yep," Nick said. "The guy with the nose and night vision should lead the way."

They reached the dining room doorway. Then Nick smelled something else. Burnt meat. He turned back to the kitchen and sniffed, but there was no trace of the scent there.

"What's wrong?" Vanessa mouthed.

He shook his head. If it was what it smelled like, he wasn't telling her until absolutely necessary. He rounded the corner into the dining room. She covered him with her gun. He paused and inhaled, picking up only the smells of blood and burnt flesh. He started forward again. He was approaching the next doorway when a board creaked. He stopped and glanced back at Vanessa. She was poised in the kitchen doorway—standing on ceramic tile.

Just as he started to move, he heard the brush of a stockinged foot. It came from the left. He turned to see another doorway, this one with stairs beyond it. A second swish of fabric on wood. Too far away to be the hall. It came from the other rooms, then, on the opposite side of the house.

As he heard the noise a third time, he remembered a similar sound, only a few hours ago. Tina dragging herself along the floor.

He could definitely smell blood. Had Malcolm repeated his trick? Nick motioned Vanessa to stay back. There was no impulse to throw caution aside and race in, not even after seeing Tina's horrible death. He'd known Tina. He didn't know these people; their deaths weren't worth taking a risk. So maybe, he thought, he was a little more like Clay than he figured. A little more wolf, at least.

He backed them into the kitchen and looked around. There was a second door, closed. He'd noted it earlier and presumed it led to the basement, but he should have checked. He was sure Vanessa would have, under other circumstances, but she was still partly shell-shocked. As soon as he looked at that closed door, though, she cursed under her breath. She motioned that she'd guard the open doorway into the dining room while he checked it.

Nick eased the door open. It led to a home office. There was a second door, cracked open leading to the other side of the house. That was where the noises came from.

Nick inhaled. A man's scent permeated the office. Stokes' office. The smell was ingrained enough that if Stokes himself was lying just beyond the room, Nick wouldn't know it. He did not, however, detect any other scents. No sign of Malcolm then.

He backed up and told Vanessa his plan.

Fourteen

NICK

ICK WAITED WHILE Vanessa got in position near the office door. As he went back through the dining room, he caught a shuffle of movement, loud enough for a human to detect. That was Vanessa, announcing her position. Whoever was in the house, it would lure him in her direction.

Nick moved silently through to the front hall. The stairs were to his right, the entry door to his left. He paused and inhaled. Definitely more of Malcolm's scent here. Two trails. One led back the way he'd come. The other went upstairs.

Nick slipped to the foot of the stairs. The stink of blood was stronger there and seemed to come from upstairs. He retreated. A leaded glass door led into a formal living room.

Malcolm's trail didn't cross its threshold. When Nick listened, though, he caught the brush of fabric on wood again, from that part of the house. Heading toward Vanessa.

He peered through the leaded glass. Werewolf night vision didn't help with that, and he had to crack open the door. He inhaled. No sign of any recent scent other than the home-owners. No blood, either. Yet he did detect the burnt flesh smell, which gave him pause. Either Richard or Sharon Stokes *was* here, injured and moving toward Vanessa. That burnt smell... Although Sharon Stokes was a half-demon, her power was minor hearing enhancement, not fire. Which meant the smell... Nick didn't want to consider what that meant.

He eased through the doorway and crossed the big living room. On the other side, if his calculations were right, lay the home office. The door leading into it was half open.

Nick moved on the far side of that door, where he couldn't be spotted. The room had gone silent. Every few minutes, Vanessa would make a soft, seemingly accidental sound. But when she did, there was no answering sound from the office, which seemed to confirm his suspicion. Whoever they were dealing with wasn't in any shape to deal with them.

He reached the half-open door and angled for a glance through. No sign of a figure. His gaze dropped to the floor. There were a few hard-to-see spots, but he could make out enough to be sure someone wasn't lying down there.

Nick took a deep breath. Yes, he definitely smelled Stokes. So where was he?

Nick's gaze surveyed the floor. Then he spotted it. An area of darkness beside the desk, with a sleeve protruding from it, the rest of the body tucked back in the shadows.

One last quick glance around and he started forward, moving quickly toward the desk, ready to find—

It was a sweater that had fallen off the back of the chair.

A faint click sounded behind him. Nick wheeled as a closet door swung open, a gun rising. He dove, and the bullet hit the wall beside him. The gun fired again while Nick lunged. The bullet sliced through the back of his shirt as he dropped and hit his assailant in the knees. Another shot. This one from across the room. He heard a raspy inhalation from above. His attacker fell, his gun sailing off to the side. Vanessa snatched it up as Nick pounced on his fallen foe.

The man had twisted as he fell and now lay on his stomach. Blood seeped from his left sleeve, where Vanessa's bullet had hit his arm.

"It's Stokes," Vanessa said. "Grab his hands so he can't cast."

A sorcerer casts with a combination of words and gestures. If the guy knew any witch magic, though, restraining him wouldn't help. As Nick caught the man's hands, he braced for a spoken spell, but Stokes only grunted in pain when Nick yanked on his injured arm.

Why hadn't Stokes cast something earlier? Sure, he had a gun, but a trained killer would use every weapon in his arsenal. Nick knew there were sorcerer spells like knock-backs and blurs that would have made Stokes' closet attack much more effective.

Then there was that smell... Even stronger now, as Nick pinned Stokes. One split second of "what did Malcolm do?" passed through his mind. Then he knew. And his stomach clenched.

He grabbed Stokes by the shoulder and flipped him over. The man didn't react to the pain now. Nick could see why he'd barely reacted after the shot. His eyes were glazed over. Dulled by painkillers. There was blood on his mouth. And that burnt smell blasted out on his breath.

"Richard Stokes," Vanessa said, walking over, gun still trained. "Were you expecting someone else tonight? Is that why your alarm was off? You were lying in wait for Malcolm?"

"Malcolm's already been here," Nick said. "And Stokes can't answer. Malcolm cut out his tongue."

Vanessa rocked back before catching herself. She quickly recovered that blank professional expression, but she couldn't mask the horror in her eyes.

"For snitching," she murmured. "He cut it out for snitching."

"With the added bonus that it robs Stokes of his power."

He released Stokes' hands and started to rise. Out of the corner of his eye, he saw something flash. A knife. Nick wheeled, but Vanessa was already in motion, grabbing Stokes' wrist, her fingers blazing. Stokes let out a grunt, more surprise than pain, as he dropped the knife. Before Nick could react, Vanessa had Stokes pinned on his stomach again, hands behind his back. She motioned for Nick to hold them while she used plastic cuffs.

"You're fast," he said.

A shaky laugh. "It's coming back. Slowly." She kicked Stokes between the shoulder blades, hard enough to make Nick wince.

"We aren't here to hurt you," Nick said, walking around to Stokes' head. "Malcolm's gone. We're on his tail. I'm sorry he did this to you."

Hate blazed through the man's drug-bleary eyes. This wasn't an innocent victim, Nick reminded himself. As much as that horrible injury made him want to feel pity, Stokes almost certainly deserved it. From what Vanessa had said, he'd made a very good partner for Malcolm. Equally vicious and ruthless.

"I'm—" Nick began to introduce himself, but Stokes cut him short with a guttural growl.

Stokes jabbed his chin at the desk and, with his hands bound, managed to mimic writing. Nick got a paper and pen.

"You're right-handed, I take it?" Vanessa said.

He nodded. She undid the cuff, and tied his left hand to the desk leg. He didn't like that—clearly he expected to sit up and write his message, but after some glowers failed to move Vanessa, he snatched the page and started to scribble a message. He wrote it in a combination of text and haphazard shorthand that Nick deciphered as: *Want my help? Find my wife. He hurts her? I'll hunt you down and do worse than cut out your goddamned tongues.*

"Charming," Vanessa said. "Your bravado is admirable, Stokes, but you're an idiot if you think you should threaten someone with a gun at your head."

He scrawled. *Find my wife or no Malcolm. I'll hunt him down and you'll never find him.*

"All right," Vanessa said. "So Malcolm took your wife—"

He cut her short with a wave and wrote. *He said someone would come for him, and if I didn't kill whoever came...*

He stopped there. Nick didn't care to imagine what Malcolm said he'd do to Sharon Stokes. The look in Stokes' eyes was enough. As soon as he read the words, though, Nick stopped and looked up, toward the upstairs, and that sick feeling in his gut returned.

Shit. Oh, shit. He wouldn't...

Hell, yes, he would. He absolutely would.

"Did you see Malcolm leave with your wife?" Nick asked.

The haunted pain in Stokes' eyes vanished in a snap, his lip curling, as if to say "What a fucking pointless question."

Nick repeated it and waved at the pad. Stokes wrote, pen strokes hard now, anger and frustration mounting.

If you're asking if I stood at the fucking window and saw which way they went—

"No, I'm…" Nick struggled for a way to word the question that wouldn't reveal his suspicion. "Malcolm did that to you. And then what? Was your wife with him? Was she conscious? Did he drag her out? I'm a werewolf, and I need some idea of what kind of trail I'm looking for. Walk me through it—quickly—so I can go after them."

Stokes still simmered, and it was obvious he considered Nick a flaming idiot, but that idiot was the guy he was counting on to bring his wife back alive. He wrote quickly, the words nearly illegible in his haste.

Broke in. Knocked her out. Knew I'd been talking to the Nasts. Said I set him up. Told what he'd do if I didn't kill whoever came here after him. Then he cut out my tongue and cauterized it. I passed out. When I woke, they were gone.

Taking Stokes' wife was too much trouble. That was the problem. One Nick wasn't about to explain to this mutilated killer, seething with rage, frantic for his wife's safety.

"I need to go upstairs," Nick said to Vanessa.

Now Stokes didn't bother with the paper. He didn't need to. Nick could decipher his garbled words just fine.

"What the fuck? No. *Fucking no,*" Stokes said as he jabbed his free hand at the door, telling them to go, get on his wife's trail, bring her back.

"I really need to go upstairs," Nick said. "To check her scent."

Vanessa knew what he was really checking. He saw that in the fresh dismay in her eyes.

As Nick headed up the stairs, the smell of blood grew stronger. He could tell himself it was from cutting off Stokes' tongue. It wasn't. The smell was much too strong for that.

The stairs led to a wide hall with four doors plus a double set that presumably led to a linen closet. Nick went into the open door first. The master bedroom, stinking of fear and sweat and blood and burnt flesh. This was where Malcolm had done it, surprising the couple as they slept.

The sheets were soaked in blood. On the floor lay the remains of Stokes' tongue, tossed aside. Nick walked to the bed. While it was a lot of blood, it wasn't enough for what he'd smelled.

Nick backed out and checked the double-doors. As he expected, it was a linen closet—a walk-in one, but still small enough to search with a visual sweep. The next door led to a spare bedroom that looked as if it'd never been used. The only trails entering were old. A bathroom was next. Also empty. Then the third bedroom, which seemed to be a second office, smelling of Sharon Stokes. No blood, though.

Nick returned to the hall and looked around. He could mentally map out the upper level and tell that all space was accounted for. The blood, however, was not.

He walked to the middle of the hall, trying to pinpoint the location of the scent, but that didn't help. It seemed to come from all directions. He crouched again, to follow Malcolm's trail. As soon as he bent, the smell grew fainter. He rose. Stronger.

Nick looked up. There, in the ceiling, was an attic door.

Fifteen

NICK

ICK WALKED UNDER the attic door and saw a strap. When he opened the hall closet, he found a hook hanging on the wall. Using it, he tugged down the pull strap. A good yank, and the attic door opened, steps sliding out with it.

As he climbed those steps, there was no doubt the blood scent came from up there. The attic was nearly pitch dark, though, and he had to pause for his eyes to adjust to the light coming from the hall below.

The attic was empty. Completely empty. Whatever the Stokes had brought with them when they moved, it obviously all fit elsewhere.

With no obstacles to block his view, Nick didn't have to move from the top of the steps to scan the entirety of the massive open space. And to assure himself there was nothing up here. Nothing but the smell of blood.

He walked out into the attic. It didn't take long before he spotted the blood pool, glistening on the dust-covered floor. When he stopped next to it, and his footsteps subsided, he picked up a sound. A very soft *plink*. Then silence.

He circled the blood pool. It was perfectly formed, with no footsteps leading from it, no empty spots inside, no sign that whoever bled here had crawled or been taken away. Yet there was clearly not a body.

Plink.

This time he saw the drop hit the pool. He looked up and saw only the black roofline above. When he blinked, his night vision adjusted and—

"Shit."

She was on the ceiling. Sharon Stokes. Spread eagled above him, her throat and wrists bloodied.

Nick took out his phone and shone the light up at Sharon's body. Only then could he see how she'd been fastened there, and when he did, his stomach lurched. He lowered the light and noticed the tools hidden in the shadow by the wall. A nail gun and a ladder.

Malcolm nailed her to the ceiling, cut her throat and let her bleed out, hanging there.

Had she regained consciousness? God, he hoped not.

He stared up at that body, and there was a part of him that couldn't quite believe it. Yes, the Malcolm he'd known was a sadistic son of a bitch, but this? What had the Nasts done to him? Nick wasn't sure he wanted to know—for now, it was enough to understand what he was dealing with…if he could.

● ● ●

NICK FOUND VANESSA and Stokes where he'd left them. Stokes lay on his stomach, both hands fastened again. Vanessa stood over him with a gun.

"Your wife's gone," Nick said.

Stokes screwed up his face, and Nick knew what he'd say if he could. *Of course she's gone, you fucking moron. That's what I told you.*

"I mean she's dead. Malcolm killed her before he left."

Stokes went still. That look of horror started to return, then it vanished, his face hardening as he bucked up, managing to get to his knees. Nick motioned for Vanessa to leave him be. He might have little sympathy for what Malcolm did to Stokes, but he felt it now, for his wife.

When Stokes pushed to his feet, he lunged at Nick. Vanessa grabbed his bound hands and yanked him back. He shook her off and settled for glaring at Nick with all the hate he could muster as he mouthed "Liar."

"I wish I was," Nick said. "But think about it. You know Malcolm. Is he really going to bother taking a hostage? All that mattered was convincing you to kill us for him."

He could see in Stokes' hesitation that he knew Nick was right. He just didn't want to believe it. And he had reason not to—if Nick claimed Sharon was dead, there was nothing stopping Stokes from helping him find Malcolm. If anything, he'd have more incentive.

"Where is she?" Stokes mouthed.

When Nick didn't answer fast enough, Stokes figured it out. He turned toward the living room. Nick moved to swing into Stokes' path, but Vanessa stopped him.

"Let him go," she murmured. "He's not giving us what we need until he sees for himself."

"I know," Nick said. "But…" He lowered his voice. "He shouldn't see her like that."

"It's bad?" Vanessa whispered.

Nick nodded, grim-faced. He broke into a jog to catch up with Stokes, already cresting the top of the stairs.

"You don't want to do this," Nick called as he loped up behind him. "Let me bring her to you."

Stokes was on the extended attic steps. Nick grabbed for his pant leg as he ascended. Stokes wheeled and kicked. Nick caught his leg. Stokes yanked, managing to keep his balance with his bound hands, but barely, ready to topple at any moment.

"Let him go," Vanessa said.

Nick looked at her. He wanted to haul Stokes' ass down those stairs, pin him on the damned floor and tell him he wasn't seeing his wife that way. That no matter what a vicious asshole Stokes was, he obviously loved her, and that shouldn't be his final memory of her.

But he knew if Elena was here, she'd say the same thing as Vanessa. Their goal was Malcolm. The sooner they went after him, the better.

He released Stokes. The man stumbled up the stairs. It was pitch black up there for anyone without werewolf night vision, and for a moment, Nick felt a surge of satisfaction.

Stokes didn't pause, though. He strode to the wall and flipped a switch with his teeth. A row of lights flickered on as Nick climbed the steps. Stokes saw the blood immediately. He walked to it, gaze tripping across the floor, looking for her. When he reached the edge of that perfect puddle, he turned and glared at Nick, as if to say "Where the hell is she?"

Nick crossed his arms and glared back. Beside him, Vanessa inhaled sharply. Stokes heard. He looked at her and followed her gaze and...

Silence. For at least ten seconds there was silence. Then Stokes screamed, a horrible, wordless scream of rage. He wheeled on Nick and if his hands hadn't been bound, Nick was certain he would have tried to kill him.

Instead Stokes stood there, bristling like an enraged boar.

"Get her down," he mouthed.

"Fuck you," Nick said.

Stokes charged. Nick slammed him in the gut and sent him flying, coughing and choking. He hit the floor. Nick advanced on him.

"I told you she was dead. I offered to get her down before you saw her. I'm not doing it now. If you want revenge, then tell us whatever you can about Malcolm. Then we'll cut you loose, and *you* can get her down."

Stokes snarled and raged, but Nick didn't budge. Yes, it would be a mercy to get Sharon down for him. It wasn't just that Stokes didn't deserve mercy. It was a question of dominance. Despite being bound at gunpoint, Stokes clearly considered himself the alpha dog here. Nick was an idiot. Vanessa was a woman. They'd damn well better jump when he said jump. And if they did, he'd see no reason to give them what they wanted.

So Nick watched Stokes rage, and stood there, waiting, until his anger and grief began to sputter.

"Let me repeat myself," Nick said. "You tell us what we want. We let you go. You take her down. Otherwise, we walk out of here, and I pick up Malcolm's trail on my own, and you can figure out how the hell you're going to call for help without the use of your hands or tongue."

Stokes struggled in his cuffs, but Vanessa had bound him well.

Nick turned for the door. Stokes lunged for him. Nick spun, caught him in the gut with another right and left him on the floor, heaving for breath.

They made it halfway down the main stairs before Stokes came after them and gestured that, yes, he'd tell them what he could.

Sixteen

NICK

T HEY LET STOKES sit at the desk and type on his laptop—a quicker way to communicate. He said that Malcolm had come by earlier that day, as they knew. He wanted Stokes' help, though of course, he claimed he was "offering him an opportunity." Stokes played along.

Malcolm needed money. He'd mooched some from Stokes already, but he was smart enough to see the income stream wouldn't last forever and he'd lose a valuable ally if he kept at it. So he'd found a job on his own. He called it assassin work; Stokes called it thug work.

The job was lucrative, though, and Stokes had expressed interest. He'd asked for details and gotten enough to be sure the job was feasible. Stokes said he'd consider it, and they made plans to meet the next day. Then Malcolm left the house, with Tina on his tail, and that's when it all went wrong.

Stokes didn't know where Malcolm was staying, but he listed a few hotels of the sort Malcolm favored these days, upper-end but not luxurious, balancing his budget with his ego. He provided the make of the car Malcolm was driving, but he was certain Malcolm would have ditched it by now. Stokes had taught him a few things about being a hired killer.

They asked for details about the job, then, as another route to Malcolm.

West coast client, Stokes typed. *No name. Sorcerer. Suspect he runs a cut-rate Cabal-wannabe operation.*

Nick looked at Vanessa.

"There are a few dozen of them," she said. "Anything from million-dollar operations to borderline street gangs."

Expect this one to be in the middle, Stokes wrote. *Up-and-comers. Malcolm said—*

Stokes stopped. Nick looked toward the window. He could pick up the distant wail of a siren. He'd been too preoccupied to notice the faint sound sooner.

Vanessa motioned subtly for Nick to check it out. "Keep going," she said to Stokes. "What did Malcolm say?"

Nick walked through to the next room. He could pick up the sirens better.

"Ambulance," he called back softly. "Midnight heart attack maybe. I'll take a look."

It was impossible to get any kind of wide view from the front windows. Nick walked to the entry door. The outside lights had been on when they arrived. He flicked them off and eased open the door. He could hear the siren, coming steadily closer. And more now, engines and tires. More than one vehicle. There was a second siren too, harder to identify.

Fire engine?

Uh, yeah. What was the chance of a fire in the neighborhood right now?

Pretty good…if Malcolm set it to draw attention to Stokes' house. To frame his former partner for murder.

But that was a roundabout way of doing things. Malcolm was never roundabout. If that's what he wanted to do, he'd just call and report someone was seriously injured—

"Shit!"

Nick raced back into the house. As he did, he heard Vanessa tell Stokes to, "Sit your ass down in that chair." He hurried through the living room. Vanessa was arguing with Stokes, her back to Nick, gun pointed at Stokes, who was standing.

"We need to—" Nick began.

She glanced over her shoulder. Stokes tensed. Before Nick could say a word, Vanessa had twisted back to her target, but Stokes was already in flight. Stokes grabbed her in a chokehold and went for the gun. Most people would keep a grip, try to somehow shoot the person behind them. Which would be nearly impossible, and Vanessa knew it.

She had the chamber open, emptying the gun so deftly that Nick heard the cartridges hit the ground at the same time he saw her toss the gun aside. Then she clamped down on Stokes' arm with ten blazing fingers. He snarled, but either the painkillers hadn't worn off or he just didn't give a shit.

Stokes backed up, his arm tightening around Vanessa's neck, her eyes bulging. Nick could smell her fingers burning into his arm, but he didn't relax his hold. Not until Nick had him in his own chokehold.

"What the hell do you think you're doing?" Nick said. "The cops are on their way. Malcolm called them in. We're trying to save your ass."

Vanessa wrenched free, gasping as she spoke. "He doesn't want to be saved. He wants us to decide he's too much trouble and put him down."

Nick looked at her as she struggled to catch her breath.

"His wife is dead upstairs," Vanessa said. "He knows Malcolm will have framed him as his final revenge—hopefully exacted *after* Stokes has helpfully killed us. But his timing was a little off."

Nick gave Stokes a shove. "You need to run. Just don't try running with us."

Vanessa grabbed up her gun and slapped it back together as she asked, "How far off are they?"

"Maybe a couple of blocks. We'll need to—"

Stokes snatched the knife from earlier. Nick wheeled, ready to block his attack. Only he didn't attack. He drew the knife back and plunged it into his heart.

Nick lunged for him, but Vanessa grabbed the back of his shirt.

"He was going to do it," she said. "It was just a question of whether he took us along."

"But the cops wouldn't have thought he cut out his own tongue."

"Doesn't matter. Malcolm wasn't letting him walk out of this. Now let's hope *we* can."

She hurried through the kitchen door. Nick followed.

●　●　●

"Wait," Vanessa said. "Wait..."

Nick could point out that he hadn't given any indication that he planned to do anything *except* wait. They were in the yard behind the Stokes house. They could just make a run for it easily from here...if their rental car wasn't parked five doors down. They couldn't abandon it. Vanessa had rented it using an untraceable account, but it still had their luggage—with fingerprints—in the trunk.

So they were waiting for a chance to run through the rear yards. The ambulance had indeed stopped at the Stokes house. So had two police cruisers. The cops had gone in first and called to the paramedics, presumably when they found Stokes dying on the study floor.

The trick here was to time their departure just right. Wait until everyone was in the house dealing with the situation and then run.

One pair of officers had circled the property. A perfunctory search. Stokes had obviously stabbed himself. It wouldn't even be clear that there'd been an intruder until they realized their victim was missing his tongue.

Now the officers had stepped inside. Vanessa was holding off, making sure they didn't immediately pop back out to check something they'd missed. Hence the, "Wait... wait..."

"Still clear?" she whispered.

"Yep."

"Any sirens?"

"Everything's fine," he said. "I'd tell you otherwise."

"All right then. Let's go."

Nick steered them through this yard and the next. There were fences to scale and it was obvious Vanessa was out of practice, but she didn't pretend otherwise, letting Nick help her as they went.

At the halfway point, Nick stayed on the fence after he'd helped Vanessa down. He rose, balancing, to get a look back at the Stokes house. It wasn't exactly a clear angle, but he could see enough of the road to be sure no new vehicles had joined the others stopped at the Stokes house. As he readied himself to jump down, though, he caught the sound of police sirens— coming from the same direction they needed to go.

Nick crouched on the fence as two cars pulled in with the others. Two detectives went inside. Two uniforms stayed on the front lawn.

He jumped down and told Vanessa.

"They're guarding against curious neighbors," she said. "They may have shut off the lights and sirens before they pulled in, but people will have heard them. Any minute now, every occupied home here will have someone peering out, trying to see what's going on. Which means we need to move. Fast. Nosy neighbors are worse than cops."

They set out side by side as they jogged across the back of the yards, both on alert for lights. They'd got through one when it seemed as if half the neighborhood lit up. When a door opened in the yard they were crossing, they dove behind the shed.

"Go on," a voice muttered, thick with sleep. "Be quick about it, Mitzie."

Nick swore.

Vanessa whispered, "We're fine. City dogs are used to people nearby, and any pooch named Mitzie isn't going to be a world-class guard dog."

"Doesn't matter," Nick whispered back. "Not when one of us is a werewolf."

He'd barely finished before the dog started wailing louder than the damned sirens. Vanessa was right about one thing—Mitzie was no guard dog. She'd caught one whiff of Nick and started throwing herself against the door to be let back in before the monster devoured her.

"Go," he whispered to Vanessa. "Take the lead."

"I'm jumping the rear fence," she said.

By going over the back, they could stay blocked by the shed. And they were blocked from Mitzie's door, now open, her owner muttering, "What the hell?" as the dog barreled inside. As soon as Nick topped the fence, though, a deck light turned on in the yard he was climbing *into*. A figure appeared at the window.

"Go!" he called down to Vanessa.

Nick jumped. He heard a muffled shout from inside the house and knew he'd been spotted.

Nick made a run for it—in the opposite direction. Over the side fence. Then over the back one. Through the yard where Mitzi's owner had, thankfully, retreated indoors to tend to his distraught pet. Over the next fence. Finally into the yard of the empty house where they'd parked.

Vanessa had the car running and the garage door up. He raced around to the passenger side and jumped in.

"Go!" he said, when she looked over at him.

"The neighbor saw you run into this yard," she said. "If we back out now—"

"I went the other way around." He rolled down the window. "The witness will tell the cops I ran *toward* the Stokes house. Now go."

Seventeen

NICK

WITH THE HEADLIGHTS off, the car rolled down the driveway. More lights flicked on in the house next door as whoever saw him in the yard figured out what to do about it. They were driving away when Nick, craning to look back, finally saw the front door open and a woman stepped out, looking toward the police cars.

"We're clear," he said.

The road dipped, and they were out of sight of the house within minutes. Once Nick was sure none of the cruisers was going to come ripping after them, he pulled his knee up, rubbing his calf and wincing.

"I think I pulled something back there," he said. "Five fences in five minutes. I'm too old for that shit."

Vanessa gave a shaky laugh. "Five fences in *twenty* minutes was too much for me. I've been too old for this shit for a while. Out of practice, too. I need to get out in the field more. I can't believe Stokes got the jump on me back there."

"You handled it," Nick said. "And he *is* a professional killer."

She screwed up her nose, as if to say, "That's no excuse." Nick watched her as she drove, her gaze fixed ahead. She was a beautiful woman. That was almost certainly not what should be going through his mind at the moment. He blamed the excitement of their escape. Still, it wasn't a, "God, she's gorgeous, and I want to pull over and jump her" kind of appreciation. Although, now that he thought of it, with his adrenalin still pumping...

No. That wasn't what he'd been thinking, and he wasn't going to think it now.

Vanessa cast an anxious glance in the rearview mirror.

"I'll hear anyone coming after us," Nick said. "My window's cracked open."

"I know."

"We're fine." He paused. "Relatively speaking."

She gave a tight laugh and loosened her death grip on the wheel, flexing her hands, only to squeeze it again with both hands, her gaze fixed into the night.

"You know what we need?" he said. "A drink."

"Oh, yeah."

"Think we can find one at…" He checked his watch. "Three-thirty in the morning?"

She glanced over. "You're serious?"

"I am. We've made our getaway. We aren't going to catch Malcolm tonight. We need to rest and convey our updates to our respective bosses…and then we need a drink. Or three."

Her laugh loosened then, as did her grip on the wheel. "If you really are serious, I won't argue. I'm sure we could find a corner store and grab—"

A phone buzzed.

"Speaking of bosses," Nick said. "That must be yours."

"Um, no. My ringer's off. When I'm in the field, I can't even put it on vibrate."

"Well, mine *is* on vibrate and…"

He trailed off as they looked at each other. Nick whipped around, clicking his seat belt off as he looked in the back seat. The phone kept ringing. He pinpointed the sound, coming from under his seat. He reached down, feeling around until his fingers touched plastic.

He pulled the phone out. A blocked number showed on the screen. He was about to answer when Vanessa grabbed the phone from him and yanked the wheel, braking hard, but not before the car lurched up over the curb.

"Out!" she said. "Now!"

She scrambled out. He followed. The phone kept ringing. Then, as the car doors slammed shut behind him, the ringing grew muffled, and he realized she'd left the phone in the car. She prodded him until they were fifty feet away.

"Cell phones are used to set off bombs," she said, before he could ask.

They stood on the curb and watched the car, still running. They were on the edges of the suburb now. A lone truck slowed as it approached. Vanessa waved her own cell phone, telling him it was fine, they'd called a tow truck.

The other phone kept ringing.

"We're assuming Malcolm put it in there, right?" Nick said. "That he looped back to watch Stokes' house, found the car—or saw us drive in—and planted it. I was in too big a hurry jumping into the car to notice his scent in the garage."

She nodded.

"Is there any other explanation?" he asked.

"No, it's Malcolm."

"Okay, then. I can't guarantee anything, but I'm ninety-nine percent sure it's not a bomb. He'd never use one."

Vanessa shook her head, gaze still trained on the car. "Anyone can adapt—"

"Not Malcolm. He really is an old dog. Using a bomb is a trick he couldn't learn even if he wanted to, and believe me, he wouldn't want to."

The phone stopped ringing. A few seconds of silence passed. Another car slowed. Vanessa waved it on. The phone started again.

"He's trying to make contact," Nick said. "That's his style. Engage the enemy." He looked around. "And the alternative is that we leave the car running, with our stuff in it, while we walk away." He looked at her. "You stay here while I check the phone—"

"No. I might be able to tell if it's been tampered with."

Nick followed her back to the car. She flung open the passenger side, then backpedaled, as if ready to dive out of the way. When no explosion came, she retrieved the phone and ran, smacking into him before waving him back. Presumably, if there was a bomb, it was in the car not the phone. So they got fifty feet away again. Then Vanessa held the phone out gingerly, turning it over in her hands as it continued to ring.

"Stand back," she said.

Nick did, only because he knew she wouldn't answer otherwise. Once he was about ten feet away, she hit the talk button.

"Hello."

Nick could hear the voice on the other end, and it was as chilling as picking up Malcolm's scent, like being sucked into a time warp back to a place you'd rather never visit again.

"Please put Nicholas on the phone," Malcolm said.

"I don't know who you—"

"Don't play coy, my dear. It makes you sound stupid. I was in your car. I smelled him. I'm sure he's right there. Just look around. Handsome fellow. Terribly charming. Not too bright."

Nick resisted the urge to scowl at that. If—like Stokes—Malcolm considered Nick an idiot, it would only make him easier to catch.

Vanessa looked at Nick. He held out his hand. There was no sense dragging this out.

"Hello, Malcolm," he said.

"Nicky. How are you, boy?"

Not exactly a boy anymore, but Nick knew that wasn't what Malcolm meant. The name, like the diminutive, was meant to put Nick in his place.

"So where is he?" Malcolm asked.

"Where's who?"

Malcolm laughed. "Really? Are you that dense, boy? Your partner-in-crime. The brains *and* the brawn."

"If you mean Clay, he's at home. Probably sleeping."

Another laugh, infused with impatience now. "Do you expect me to believe that? There's no way he'd send his puppy out alone. I remember when you were boys, how you followed him around, just like a puppy. And as helpless as one. Clayton's not only your friend. He's your protector. If you're there, he's nearby. Guaranteed."

"Would you like to wager on it?" Nick paused. "I've got a new car. A Jag. I remember you liked Jags. Mine's top of the line. If Clay's here, you can have it. I bet you'd like that. Not a lot of fancy cars in your life these days."

Silence. Considering whether to call Nick's bluff? Fuming at the dig about his finances? Or just shocked that Nick actually had a comeback?

"Yes," Nick said. "Clay looked after me when I was young, because he was a werewolf long before I was. And, yes, that isn't the only reason. I'm not my father. I'm no warrior. But I'm not a boy anymore either, and neither is Clay. His mate is the Alpha. He has children. Do you really think he's going to come running after you? Do you really think you're worth it?"

More silence. Then a laugh. "Yes, I do, because I saw his face at Nast headquarters. He's not going to let me live out my retirement in peace."

"No, he's going to kill you. But first you need to be found, and that's really more trouble than he's willing to expend on you."

Now Nick was certain Malcolm's silence masked seething. He glanced at Vanessa. She looked anxious and motioned he might not want to antagonize Malcolm. Nick knew what he was doing. No way in hell would Malcolm leave town if Clay wasn't here. Run from Nick Sorrentino? That was just humiliating.

"Clay may have given you his grunt work," Malcolm said after a minute. "But I think he'll want to come now. You're in over your head, Nicky."

"Because you killed three people tonight? Slaughtering humans is par for the course with you, Malcolm. Unless you've got a posse at your command, you like easy prey."

"Oh, it isn't me you need to worry about, Nicky. Not right now. It's the guys on the other end of the GPS in that phone you're holding."

Nick went quiet.

Malcolm chuckled. "That shut you up. Let me help, or you'll be there all night figuring it out. Those three werewolf hunters you saw earlier are just one team on the prowl. There are two others, and they're all in Detroit. And someone has helpfully provided them with the GPS in that phone. So you have two choices. Either you run back home to Daddy or you call Clayton and his bitch to come rescue you. Because otherwise—"

Tires squealed a couple of blocks over.

"In the car!" Nick said as he smacked the phone off. He drew his arm back to pitch it, but Vanessa grabbed his elbow.

"They're tracking the GPS," he said. "He gave it to the werewolf hunters. Three teams of them."

She took the phone from him. "Then we'll have better luck throwing them off track *with* this. Get in and drive."

Eighteen

NICK

NICK PEELED OFF the curb and hit the gas, but it wasn't exactly the sort of car he was used to, and when he looked into his rearview mirror, he could see a pickup bearing down on them.

"I've got their license number," Vanessa said. "That might help later for ID, but right now, we need to lose them. Stay on the straightaway."

"But they're gaining—"

"Not fast enough, and this is no deserted back road. They'll follow until they can find a place to push us off the street. Just give me two minutes to scramble this."

"Scramble?"

"The signal. That won't help with these guys, but it'll keep the other two teams from catching up."

He glanced over. She had her kit and was doing something to the phone. He turned his attention back to the pickup. Vanessa was right—the truck got about three car lengths behind them and stayed there. While the road wasn't busy, the occasional other vehicle meant their pursuers weren't taking a chance. They were waiting for Nick to veer down a quiet side road.

"And…got it," Vanessa said. "They'll still see a signal, but it'll send them on a wild goose chase. Can you lose these guys?"

"In this car?"

She chuckled. "It's not a Jag, there's a distinct advantage to having an ordinary car—it's much easier to lose them. Do you want to switch spots?"

He glanced over.

"We can do it," she said. "I have before. Mid-car-chase driver switch." A flashed grin. "It's fun."

"I'll take your word for it. I'm fine with driving. You navig—"

The truck shot forward, narrowing the gap between them.

"Um…" Nick began.

"Damn it," Vanessa said, twisting to watch the truck. "The idiots are getting restless. Can you go any faster?"

142

"I can. But *that's* the problem." He waved at the red light ahead—with cars going through.

"Make a hard right at the light. Join the traffic flow. Try not to hit anyone."

The last part was the toughest. The road ahead wasn't jam-packed, but a car passed every few seconds.

"Nick! Brace—!"

The pickup bumped them. Nick smacked against the seat belt. He hit the accelerator. The light ahead was still red, with no sign it'd turn green anytime soon. Nick played with the acceleration, easing back and jolting forward, judging the traffic flow ahead, trying to gauge…

He hit the gas. There was a split second where the engine hesitated, as if to say, "You want me to do *what?*" Then it revved, and while they didn't exactly fly back in their seats, the car did accelerate, engine whining.

Nick glanced over his shoulder. He could see the driver's face, screwed up in confusion, the passenger's eyes wide, mouth open as he said something, likely some variation of, "Slow the fuck down!" as they barreled toward the intersection.

A glance at his own passenger showed the same expression on her face.

"You need to slow—" she began.

"Got it."

"You can't take the turn—"

"Hold on."

He gauged traffic flow, slowing just a little. Behind him, he could hear the pickup's passengers, shouting now.

"He's going through! Goddamn it, Ted, don't you dare follow—!"

Nick braked hard, sending the car into a skid, then steering out and around the corner, wide enough to make a car in the opposite lane veer. He heard the other driver yell an obscenity. Completely unwarranted, considering that Nick probably saved the guy's life, because as the driver veered, he also slowed, and the guy in the pickup—still thinking Nick was going straight through—kept going, narrowly avoiding a T-bone.

There was still plenty of honking, and a squeal of tires. Nick accelerated again, zooming up on a transport in front of him. He weaved to see past it. Then he swerved into the opposite lane—and into the headlights of an oncoming car.

"You don't have time—!" Vanessa began.

Nick hit the gas. She was right—he didn't have time. But presuming the person at the wheel wasn't asleep, the oncoming car would brake. Which it did, tires protesting as Nick's car veered in front of the truck. Both the oncoming car and the truck laid on their horns. Nick put the pedal down again, passing the next car, and then making a sharp right at the light and another at the next, taking them back the way they'd come. He crossed the first road they'd originally been on and continued into the night. The pickup was long gone.

"You *can* drive," Vanessa said. She grinned over at him, eyes sparkling, and for a second, he knew the rest of the night was forgotten.

"So, do I get that drink now?" she asked.

"Several. I think we've earned them."

Her grin grew. "We have."

They continued in silence for a few minutes. Then she said, "I need to call Rhys."

"And I need to call Elena. Just let me get where we're going."

"Which is…?"

"Someplace we can get a drink."

She smiled and relaxed in her seat. They reached the highway, and she watched out the window, saying nothing for about five minutes, and then, "We need a plan."

"I know. Just…let's rest a bit."

Nick left the highway two exits early, intentionally. He glanced over, waiting for her to ask where they were headed, but she had her eyes closed. When she opened them, ten minutes later, she shot forward in her seat.

"Why are we at the airport?" she said.

"Getting a drink. If anything's open. Then getting you on a plane home."

"Hell, no." She twisted to face him. "You are not putting me on—"

"Yep, I am."

"If this is because Stokes got the jump—"

"It's not." Nick pulled into the parking garage. "It's about the fact that we're chasing a psychopath who'll grab you the first chance he gets. Then he'll kill you—horribly—to teach me a lesson."

Her face hardened. "I'm not some date you brought along—"

"I know that." He pulled into a spot. "You're accustomed to bad guys who will kill you if you get in their way. But that's not Malcolm. He knows I'm with a woman now, and he's going to target you because I'll blame myself. That's how he operates. He kills those who don't matter. And he hurts those who do. He *will* come after you."

"Then we'll know how to catch him."

"No."

Vanessa sat there, poised, as if waiting for him to elaborate. He looked her in the eye. "No."

"Then I guess we'll have to split up and do this on our own. You call Elena and have her send Clay. I'll get Jayne and a few others, and we'll go after Malcolm separately. Then we'll pray it doesn't turn into a huge cluster-fuck, attacking each other and those damned werewolf hunters, while Malcolm circles until he can take out Clayton."

"After that fight at Nast headquarters, Malcolm knows Clay will—and can—take him down. The minute Clay's here, he'll bolt. Elena knows that. She won't send him."

"So she'll come out herself? Even better. Malcolm would love that. You said he likes to hurt his enemies."

Nick shook his head. "You're not drawing me into this argument, Vanessa. Stay or go. Your choice, but only because I can't force you onto a plane."

He left her the keys and got his bag from the trunk. Vanessa caught up with him halfway to the parking garage exit.

"I'm not trying to be a pain in the ass, Nick," she said. "But this guy killed my agent, and that gives me a reason to go after him. I can do that with my own people, but I'd really rather do it with you. You know Malcolm. Bring in whoever you want, and I'll work with them, too. But I have experience and tools that your people don't. Like checking for a security system or scrambling that phone signal."

"I don't want to take responsibility—"

"You're not *bringing* me. You're teaming up with me." When he didn't respond, she said, "How about I call Rhys? Get his word on this. If he wants to recall me, he can."

He stopped walking. "Fine. You'll make that call here where I can hear both sides. But before that, I'll phone Elena. If she insists we split up, I have to do that."

"Understood."

Nineteen

VANESSA

VANESSA WENT INTO the terminal and used the restroom while Nick phoned Elena. She could have also placed an advance call to Rhys to tell him what was up, maybe even massage the facts to be sure he'd let her stay. Nick hadn't foreseen that because he wasn't underhanded by nature. She'd given her word. He expected her to stick to it. So she'd honor that trust.

When she got back, Nick was done with his call. Elena had agreed to let Vanessa help him, if that's what Rhys wanted. In the meantime, she was driving to Detroit with Clay, ready to jump in the moment Nick needed them.

Elena's decision didn't surprise Vanessa. If Malcolm did go after Vanessa? Well, let's be perfectly objective here. That was better than risking Nick or any of her Pack. And in coming after Vanessa, he'd get close enough for Nick to act. A cold, hard assessment. And the same one Vanessa would make if an outsider volunteered to assist a member of her team.

Vanessa called Rhys next. There was another reason why she hadn't bothered to sneak a call to him earlier. Because she didn't need to. Rhys could be as hard as Elena, but he was a good leader. While she accepted the blame for Tina's death, he wouldn't let her take it. She'd argued to let Nick in sooner, and he'd refused.

She even admitted Stokes got the jump on her, since she'd have to put that in her report. He said the same thing that Nick had—Stokes was a trained killer, and she handled it fine. If she was comfortable staying, then she could stay. Like Elena, though, he wasn't sitting back to wait for an update call. Jayne and Rhys were both coming out. Like Elena and Clayton, they'd hang back and wait for a distress call.

When Rhys said he'd wait for a distress call, he meant it— part of her kit was a short-range "SOS button" with a GPS. Now that someone would be in range soon, she was expected to wear it.

● ● ●

IT WAS NOT easy to find alcohol at five in the morning. Apparently, state liquor laws meant that even the corner stores stopped selling it at 2 a.m. Or they did for most people. Nick sussed out a store with a thirty-something woman behind the counter, asked Vanessa to stay in the car, went in and came out with alcohol.

It wouldn't have to be a hard sell. Even after a night of narrow escapes and filthy buildings, all it had taken was five minutes in a restroom for Nick to look like he'd stepped off a magazine cover. Vanessa was sure with only a modicum of charm—and perhaps a generous tip—he'd been able to convince the clerk to break the rules for him.

Before he'd gone into the store, Nick had asked what she drank and she'd joked about missing her nightly gimlet. In all seriousness, she said a fifth of gin and a bottle of 7-Up would be fine. At the hotel, she discovered he'd grabbed good gin and a packet of Rose's Lime mix. While it was perfectly possible that he knew how to make the old-fashioned cocktail, Vanessa suspected he'd looked it up on his cell phone. A guy considerate enough to do that for someone he didn't particularly seem to care for? Well, they didn't make many men like that in Vanessa's world, which only made the "didn't particularly seem to care for her" part all that much harsher.

When they'd gotten on that plane together, she'd known he'd rather be with just about anyone else. His opinion seemed to have improved since then, but she suspected she'd have had to work very hard for it to get worse. Since Nick had a reputation for being nice to just about everyone...well, that didn't exactly mean he'd want her number when all this was over, not even as a professional contact. Meanwhile, the more time she spent with Nick, the more time she *wanted* to spend with him, and it had nothing to do with the fact that he was very nice to look at. Put him in a dark room, and she'd still be happy. Of course, if she was in a dark room with Nick, she'd probably be *very* happy...

Oh, hell.

She knocked back the rest of her gimlet and let Nick mix her a second. It didn't help that there was a king-size bed beside their table. The hotel had apparently been out of double beds. When she said "apparently," she wasn't implying that Nick had lied. As nice as that might have been for her ego, Nick would never pull that. She'd been the one asking when the desk clerk had said there were only king rooms left, all the while giving Vanessa a look that said, "This better be your brother, sugar, or you're out of your mind for *wanting* two beds." The room had a pullout sofa, though, and Nick had gallantly offered to take it, though she planned to flip him for it when the time came.

At least they weren't drinking in awkward silence. Nick was being his charming self, making conversation. He seemed in no rush to get to sleep, and she needed the drink as much as she'd joked she did. She was working on her third now, as he asked about her move from field work to team leader.

"I'm a half-assed field agent," she said. When he started to make the obligatory protest, she raised her hand against it. "That's not humility. I'm better suited to supervising. As you may have been able to tell, I'm not a twenty-five-year-old kickass martial-arts fighter. Never was, even *at* twenty-five. Getting through basic training was a bitch. Marksmanship? No problem. Academic? Technical? Easy-peasy. Running, jumping, climbing? Hell, no. I just don't have the body for it."

His gaze dropped, and she'd like to think he was checking out aforementioned body, just as she'd really like to think that the spark in his eyes was an appreciative assessment. When he said, "Nothing wrong with that," there was a flicker of hope that he was complimenting her, but he followed the comment with, "Not everyone's cut out for everything," and she took another gulp of her drink.

Stop acting like a schoolgirl with a crush.

Oh, but Nick Sorrentino was so crush-able. In every way.

Another long drink, this one draining her glass. He went to take it, then stopped, looking her in the eyes, head tilted, as if assessing her sobriety.

"I'm fine," she said. "I'm a big drinker."

His lips quirked in a smile. "And a lousy liar. I'm good at reading the signs, and it's time to cut you off."

"Spent some time tending bars, have you?" Even as she said it, she wanted to cuff herself. Nick Sorrentino had most certainly never been a bartender, not unless he'd played one on a friend's yacht.

Before she could retract it, he laughed and shook his head. "No, nothing like that. I'm just..." He shrugged. "Careful. If a woman's had too much..." Another shrug. "I'm careful."

In other words, he'd learned to read the signs so he wouldn't take advantage of a woman who'd overindulged.

Damn, she thought, looking at him. *Why hasn't someone snatched you up by now?*

Again, it was a stupid question. If a man like this was snatchable, some woman would have done it twenty years ago. He wasn't interested in that. Why would he be? For a guy like Nick Sorrentino, there was no upside to a committed relationship. It wasn't like he'd get more sex if he had a steady girlfriend.

And maybe, for five minutes, you could stop thinking about Nick and sex?

She reached for the gin bottle.

"I'm not going to stop you," he said. "But if you really aren't accustomed to that much, you'll pay for it tomorrow."

She took the lime mix instead, pouring herself a glass.

"We should be getting to bed." Her cheeks heated. "I mean, getting to sleep."

"I know what you meant." He cleared his throat, the easy humor falling from his eyes. "I also know you might not be comfortable sharing a room, given what you think of me."

"What?" She looked up, startled. "No, I—I have absolutely no qualms about sleeping with you." *Oh God, did she just say that?* "I mean, sleeping in the same room as you."

His head tilted again, another searching look, cooling fast now.

When he spoke, his tone was clipped, uncharacteristically formal. "If I make you nervous, I can assure you I did not suggest a single room because I plan to seduce you."

"I know that. And you didn't suggest it—we agreed on it. For safety." She forced a laugh. "It's not like you need to trick a woman into a hotel room to get laid." *Stop talking. Stop talking now.* "That didn't come out right. I just mean—"

"You made it clear this afternoon what you meant, Vanessa, and if we can avoid resuming that conversation, I'd appreciate it."

"I was flirting."

The words slipped out before she could stop them. No, not slipped. Blurted. She'd seen that she was losing any ground she'd gained and the only solution—after three gimlets— seemed to be this. Honesty.

How did she expect him to react? Blink in surprise. Laugh maybe. Relax certainly. Instead, he pulled back, gaze shuttering. He thought she was mocking him.

"I was flirting," she said. "I...Jayne and Tina...well, they talked, and I... You sounded like a nice guy."

"Nice?"

Her cheeks heated. "Among other things. I know how terrible this sounds, but I didn't know you, and it's been a while..."

"Been a while?" he repeated.

Now her cheeks seared. *Shut up. Just shut up.* But she couldn't. Not while he was looking at her. She had to get traction. Somehow.

"Sex," she blurted. "It's been a while. I've never had a one-night stand, and you seemed... I wanted..."

"Some of what I appeared to be freely offering?"

"Oh God, even plastered I know how bad this sounds. I'm sorry. I'm really sorry."

Was she imagining things or did he seem to be relaxing? A hint of a smile in his eyes? Nope, she was imagining it. She had to be.

She plowed forward. "I didn't know you. Yes, that's a lousy excuse. If you were a woman and I was a guy thinking that, it'd be wrong and insulting, so it still is, and I apologize. I'm just trying to explain why...I didn't mean to offend you this afternoon."

"You were flirting." Definitely a hint of a smile in his eyes now.

"I...I thought if I talked about you and them, you'd know I was okay with it, that I wasn't a prude or anything. I was trying to open the door."

"I see." He watched her for at least ten seconds, then burst out laughing. When he recovered, he said, "Not a lot of experience with flirting, I take it?"

"None."

"You may want to work on your technique."

She sputtered a laugh. "You think?"

They both laughed. Then Vanessa sobered. "I *am* sorry. I think you're a great guy, and that was a lousy thing to do. I was wrong to presume... Well, to presume anything. The point is that I'm not the least bit concerned that you brought me here to seduce me. You wouldn't do that, and not just because you don't need to. You'll be a gentleman because that's what you are."

He shrugged, pulling back as if uncomfortable with the compliment. "It's basic respect."

"I know. I'm just saying that I appreciate it." She forced a smile. "And that I know I have nothing to worry about, even without that 'basic respect.'"

A smile played on his lips. "Oh, I wouldn't say that. Since we're being honest, I'll admit that I possibly was playing to type this afternoon, checking you out when we met. Which doesn't mean we'd have ended up in bed. I'd like to think there's a little more to my decision-making than, 'Damn, she's hot,' but there *was* that, and I'll admit it, even if it makes me seem like exactly what you expected."

"You aren't what I expected." She met his gaze. "At all."

He pulled back again, not displeased with the implied flattery, but not comfortable with it either. He smiled and shook his head. "I think three gimlets is past your limit."

"It is." She paused. "Wait, did you say I was hot?"

He laughed. "*Definitely* past your limit. Let's get you to bed. Alone."

"Damn."

He leaned forward and she thought he was going to say something. But he kissed her. The shock of that almost made her pull back. Luckily, she recovered fast enough to return it. When she tried to put her hands around his neck, though, he caught and held them, and kept kissing her, a gentle kiss that promised more but delivered nothing. Not a teasing kiss. Not a quick buss either. Something else. Something sweet and careful, like a first kiss after a high school date, a kiss that said simply, "I like you." It also said, quite clearly, "This is all you're getting," but added a subtle "…for now."

"Time for bed," he said when he pulled back. "For sleep."

"I know. You take it. I've got the sofa."

He shook his head. "Absolutely not. I'm taking—"

She cut him off with a wave, walked over and pulled out the sofa bed. He hurried to help.

"This is mine," he said.

"Mine." She flounced down onto it and laid back. "And I'm not moving. So unless you want to share…"

His gaze travelled over her, and she swore that gaze was like gasoline, her demon fire igniting and searing a path down her body. She reached up and undid the first button on her shirt. Then the second. He watched, his breath coming faster. When she undid her front bra clasp, he yanked his gaze up to her eyes.

"You're drunk," he said.

"Doesn't matter."

A wistful smile shattered the lust in his dark eyes. "Yes, it does." He walked beside the sofa, leaned over and kissed her again, that sweet promise of a kiss. "I appreciate the offer," he said when he pulled back. "I would *love* to accept, but…"

She lifted up and kissed him, that same kiss, nothing but promise.

"Thank you," she said, then fastened her shirt and watched him retreat to his side of the room.

Twenty

NICK

WHEN NICK WOKE to sunlight streaming into the room, he bolted up, certain he'd forgotten to set his alarm for driving Noah to school. Then he saw the half-closed curtains...which were not his curtains. The night rushed back and he sat there, propped up, taking a moment to process it. Then his gaze swung to the sofa bed where Vanessa was...

The sofa bed was empty.

Now he did jump up, legs swinging out, feet hitting the floor. Had she left? Woken up sober, remembered the gimlets and the conversation and the kisses, and slipped out in embarrassment? He paused. No, Vanessa wasn't stupid. She wouldn't run off when Malcolm was on the prowl.

A noise sounded across the room. He noticed light under the bathroom door, exhaled and lay back down.

He shouldn't have kissed her. She'd been drunk and from the way she'd been blushing furiously when she admitted she'd hoped to seduce him, he had a feeling she was going to regret that kiss.

But he couldn't help himself. She'd been so flustered, so anxious to apologize, even if it meant embarrassing herself with her confession.

Last night, he'd seen many sides of Vanessa. The cool leader and the tough agent, certainly, but also the pain and grief and blame over Tina, and the blame and self-recrimination over Stokes. In spite of that, she'd been determined to see this through.

He hadn't fought very hard when Elena and Rhys decided she could stay. He still wished she'd gotten on that plane—for her own safety—but he wasn't exactly gritting his teeth and counting down the hours until they could go their separate ways.

Yet they would go their separate ways. Eventually. And there'd been a moment, lying in bed last night after kissing her, that he'd tried to figure out how to see her again. He supposed the answer was easy—just *say*, "Hey, I'd like to see you again." But he had no idea where she lived, and if she wasn't a short drive from New York, then "getting together" involved serious effort, which would imply that, well, he was serious. That wasn't a message he'd ever send. Not on so short an acquaintance.

The bathroom door opened. Vanessa walked out, dressed in her button-down shirt and, from what he could tell, nothing else. If he'd pictured how she might look the morning after sex—and yes, let's be honest, he had—this was it, her long hair mussed, falling over the half-buttoned shirt, her full breasts pushing against the fabric as she walked, her long legs bare, shirt riding up enough to give him teasing glimpses of full hips and...

And he was staring. Also...He tugged at the sheet to hide his rising interest.

"Sorry," he said, pulling his gaze away.

She smiled. "If I objected to being watched, I'd have put my pants back on."

So he watched, since that implied permission and perhaps even invitation. She walked to the side of his bed and stood there, smiling as his gaze traveled down her.

"I'm sober," she said.

"So I see."

She put one knee on the bed, her shirt riding enough to show her panties, very simple white cotton trimmed with lace, but small enough that he couldn't help thinking how they must look from the rear, if she bent over, that lush ass—

The sheet didn't really help now. He could shift, trying to hide it better, but Vanessa had her hands on the bed now, moving slowly onto it, watching him for any sign that she should retreat, and he decided hiding his interest really wasn't in his best, well, interests.

"Is this okay?" she asked, one foot still on the floor.

He glanced down, directing her gaze. When she saw the obvious tent in the sheets, she grinned, her eyes sparkling with delight and, yes, surprise, as if she somehow figured she could walk over half naked and he'd be yawning, really wishing she'd just let him sleep. If that's what she expected, she'd clearly been hanging out with men in rather desperate need of a little blue pill.

He moved over, letting her onto the bed. While she was still climbing in, he undid the remaining buttons on her blouse. It fell open. He reached in and cupped her breasts. She let out a soft hiss as his thumbs rubbed across her already-erect nipples. She shrugged off the shirt and damn, she was gorgeous, hair tumbling down over breasts he could barely get his hands around, full and soft. If it was possible to get any harder, he did, his cock pushing urgently against his briefs now, as he gripped her breasts and pulled her down into a kiss. She kissed him back—hell, how she kissed him back, nothing like last night, hard and rough and hungry, leaving no doubt where this was leading, but... As much as he hated to ask the question, he knew he had to.

"I know you're sober," he said. "But are you sure? If you've never had a one-night—"

"I shouldn't start now," she said. "I know. You're right."

Shit. He shouldn't have asked. Damn it, he shouldn't have—

But he had to, didn't he? He exhaled and started easing back. So did she. Instead of crawling off him though, she only lifted up on all fours, then leaned down to kiss him again, her hard nipples brushing his chest.

"I can't have sex with you and walk away," she said as she tugged the sheet down. "Maybe I could have, before we met, but then I got to know you and… One night—or morning—wouldn't be enough."

"I—"

"And I know you don't do more than that," she said, lowering her mouth to his chest, tongue flicking his nipples, teeth nibbling them before she raised her head. "Or a sequence of nights, equally casual."

"I—"

"I'm not asking you to say this is different. It'd be a lie, and you don't play that game." She hooked the sides of his briefs, pulling them over his hips, his cock jumping free. "You're a decent guy. Your terms are clear. Casual sex or no sex. Which means, as much as I'm going to regret it, no sex."

"I—"

"That's not an ultimatum," she said, looking up at him. "I wouldn't crawl naked into your bed and tease you into agreeing to something you don't want. I'm crawling naked into your bed to say *thanks but no thanks,* in the most appreciative way I can think of."

She shifted down, curls and breasts tickling his chest, then his thighs as she moved down over his cock, her lips parting as she lowered them to it.

"You don't have to—"

She grinned, cutting him short. "Oh, believe me. I want to," she said and went down on him.

Twenty-one

NICK

Vanessa may not have had any experience with one-night stands, but that certainly didn't mean she was inexperienced. If anything, he mused later, the fact that she was accustomed to long-term relationships seemed to actually have its benefits. You could get away with lazy or inattentive sex on a one-nighter. With a long-term partner, more skill was required...and the time to develop that skill was provided. In short, it was the best blowjob he'd had in years, and when she finished, he showed his appreciation by reciprocating, which she certainly seemed to appreciate in return.

Now they were in bed, finishing a room service breakfast and struggling to keep their attention on the topic at hand—planning their next move. Or Nick was struggling. The food had helped as a temporary distraction. He'd been starving, and since Vanessa knew what he was, he didn't have to hold back. He'd gotten two breakfasts, eaten them both, and she'd only teased about a werewolf's legendary appetite.

The meal over, they'd started planning, and that's when the food settled and he noticed Vanessa was wearing the panties and shirt again, the blouse left unbuttoned, modestly hanging almost closed, but with enough of a gap to tease whenever she moved. She looked even sexier now, sated and smoky-eyed, lounging in the bed, completely at ease.

"The problem is finding Malcolm," she said. "We can't in a city this size. We know he's around, and you suspect he'll make a move for me—"

"He will."

"Which leads to problem number two. With that phone scrambled, he's not going to find *us* either."

She shifted, blouse falling open, revealing a generous curve of breast and—

He pulled his gaze away. *Focus.* What had she been saying? Right, the phone.

"Should we unscramble it?" he said. Before she could answer, he shook his head. "No, obviously not, or it'll bring those werewolf hunters running."

"Also Malcolm would smell a trap."

"True."

She reached for her own phone, blouse stretching open now, one breast showing, nipple partly erect and—

"We kept the phone so he could call," Nick said quickly. "Can we call him? I know the number was blocked but…"

"That's just what I was checking," she said, tapping her phone. "I set someone on it last night, reverse tracing the number. Still nothing, but that's still our best bet. The trick, again, is how to work it so he doesn't smell a trap."

Nick shook his head. "No, the trick is to let him smell a trap, but one as clumsy as he expects from me. One he figures he can easily thwart."

"Okay, let me grab my book. I brainstorm better on paper."

She climbed from bed and crossed to her bag. When she bent over it, her blouse fell open and rode up to her waist, her ass on full display, those tiny white panties covering just enough to—Nick took a deep breath and tried to steer his thoughts elsewhere. It didn't work, probably because he was still looking. She rummaged through the bag, full breasts hanging free, ass moving as she shifted, inviting him to rip off those panties and—

She straightened and turned. "Okay, I—"

Her gaze dropped to his crotch, cock straining against his boxers. A slow grin. "Should I bend over again for you?"

He let out a low growl.

Her grin grew. "That legendary werewolf appetite isn't just for food, is it?"

He said nothing as she walked back to the bed, an extra swing in her hips, blouse left half open, eyes glittering with the confidence of a woman who knows a man's watching her and that he's enjoying the view immensely.

She stopped at the side of the bed. "We do need to get to work, however inconvenient the timing. That leaves two options. Either I get dressed. Or I..." Her gaze dropped to his crotch. "Take care of the problem I caused."

"I'd hate to ask you to get dressed."

She laughed, eased onto the bed and tugged down his boxers with one hand. The other hand reached in, her warm fingers wrapping around—

The phone rang. *His* phone.

"It's mine," he said as she paused. "Just ignore..." He struggled to finish the sentence. *Ignore it. Keep going.* But it could be Malcolm. Or Elena. And he shouldn't be...

Ah, shit.

"Answer," she said, pulling up his boxers. "I'll give you a rain check. Redeemable at any time, any place."

She grinned wickedly, and the thought of all the places he *could* redeem that rain check gave him pause. It also made him think whoever was calling could wait a few minutes. But Vanessa was already handing him his phone from the nightstand. When he saw the number, he swore. Reese. It *could* have waited.

No, he realized with an inward sigh, it couldn't have. Even if he'd known that it was almost certainly nothing more urgent than, "Hey, where'd you put the TV remote?" it didn't matter, because it *could* be more urgent, and there was no way he was focusing on sex while worrying about that.

He answered.

"Okay," Reese said. "I give up. I need an address."

Nick flipped to his messages, seeing if he'd missed a text. He hadn't.

"What?" he said.

"I'm breaking down and admitting that I'm a lousy detective. I can't find you. I need an address."

Nick went still. Before he could ask what the hell Reese meant—*and please don't let it be what it seems to be*—Reese continued, "I've been here for two hours. I've called every bloody four-star hotel and even a few of the threes. I've used your name and both your aliases. My master plan to show up on your doorstep has failed."

"You're in Detroit…?"

"Um, yeah. Kinda the gist of what I was saying."

"What the hell are you—?"

Nick clipped his question short. As he paused, Reese continued, talking fast, rambling, as if he could distract Nick from the why with details of the how, explaining that he'd told Antonio that Nick called and said Reese could join him on his mission, so he packed a bag and drove to Detroit overnight. He'd then spent the last few hours trying to figure out where Nick was staying.

"You told Elena, right?" Nick said. He knew the answer, but he asked anyway.

A long pause.

"Let me rephrase that," Nick said. "You *asked* Elena. That's a statement not a question, because she's the Alpha, and you would never do something like this without checking with her, and if you have, then Clay is going to kick your ass all the way back home, not just for acting without checking, but for being so damned disrespectful that you didn't even think to ask."

Silence, then a quiet, "Shit." A pause. "Should I…? I'll call her now."

"Where are you?"

"Some diner—"

"Where *exactly* are you. Name and location."

The pause seemed to get even longer this time, though the question was a simple one. "What happened?" Reese said finally.

"Give me the damned address."

Reese did.

"Now stay there. Understand? Do not leave that table, not even to take a piss. I'll be there in half an hour, and I'd damned well better find you still in that seat."

"Um, what's up?"

"Did you hear me?"

"Sure. I just…"

Reese trailed off, and Nick could hear the concern and uncertainty in his voice, as he had when Nick first demanded the address. Yes, at home, Nick set the schedules and the boundaries, and he doled out the punishments, but he never snapped orders or raised his voice.

"Just stay there," Nick said, taking it down a notch. "Whatever happens, remain in that seat."

"I will."

Twenty-two

NICK

NICK DROVE AS Vanessa gave directions from her phone. He could feel her casting worried glances his way as she'd been doing since he'd hung up and started getting dressed. She'd figured out what happened from his side of the conversation. She'd said little since. Worried he'd bite her head off, too? Thinking now that maybe he wasn't such a nice guy after all? Later, he was sure he'd regret not explaining, but right now, it didn't seem important. It couldn't be important.

"I know you're worried," she said finally.

He grunted an answer.

"I'm trying to figure out how to say this without pissing you off even more..."

"Left or right," he said, waving at the road, which ended ahead.

She checked. "Left."

Silence until he made his turn.

"It's a city of a million, Nick. I know you realize the chances of Malcolm finding him..."

She went quiet. Nick kept his gaze straight ahead, but his gut churned. If Malcolm found Reese... He clenched the steering wheel. Going after Vanessa would be a dagger to Nick's back. But Reese? That would be standing right in front of him and driving the blade through his heart. Given the choice, there was no question who Malcolm would pick.

"He won't find him," Vanessa said, her voice low. "You know that. Not this quickly. He'd need to know Reese was here, and start looking, and even then, Reese would have to do something stupid, like check into a hotel under his own name. He just got here. He drove around in his car, then he went for breakfast. Malcolm cannot find him."

Silence.

"Nick..."

He eased his foot a fraction off the pedal.

"He's Australian, right?" Vanessa said.

Nick glanced over sharply.

"I'm trying to distract you," she said. "If you want me to shut up, tell me to shut up. But this will go better if your blood pressure is lower by the time you get there. So, if you can, tell me about Reese."

He did, awkwardly at first, spitting out a few facts, then relaxing and talking—maybe even bragging. He didn't reveal anything too personal, but he did talk.

"And there are two more, right?" she said. "Morgan and Noah?"

"You did your homework."

A wry smile. "I was hoping to seduce you, remember? In retrospect, I think I'd have gotten further talking about your kids not your conquests."

"They aren't—"

"I know. They're not *your* kids. They aren't even kids, technically. But they're your family of choice."

He managed a faint smile. "I wouldn't exactly call it a choice. They landed in my lap and were stuck with me."

"But you chose to take them in. To give them a home. Three total strangers."

Nick shifted. "Noah wasn't—"

"I know. He's the son of an old friend. But you know what I mean. You just don't like taking credit."

"Because I didn't do anything to deserve it. We have money. We have a big house. I have time for them. I wanted to do this. It was my choice, and I don't think I've ever made a better one. I'm not cut out for children. I realized that when Elena and Clay had the twins. This is right for me."

A moment of silence, then she said, "Make a left up here."

He turned, then said, "You've got my background info. I don't have yours. Ever been married? Any kids?"

"No and no. Too busy for both. I have a niece who lives with me, though. Her mom died of cancer five years ago."

"I'm sorry."

"It was hard, for both of us. My sister was my best friend. Sophie and I have been close since she was born, so that helped. Dawn's death just brought us closer."

"You adopted Sophie?"

She laughed. "No, nothing like that. Dawn was five years older than me, so Sophie was past the age of needing to be adopted. She stayed with her dad until she came out to Boston U and moved in with me."

"You live in Boston?"

"I do."

He found himself mentally calculating the distance. A four-hour drive from the city, but only three from their place.

Vanessa continued, "I know, I don't have the Boston accent. I grew up in Newark. Yes, I'm a Jersey girl. I kept the hair, but I managed to lose the accent, thankfully long before that show started."

"Show?"

"If you don't know it, I'm not mentioning it. Now, you'll want to turn right at the next light. Then we're only a mile away."

He eased back into his seat. "Tell me about Sophie."

She grinned. "Happily."

She did, with as much pride as he'd talked about the boys. By the time she said, "That's it, up there on the left," he was relaxed and ready to handle the situation calmly and rationally.

"Thanks," he said as he pulled into a parking spot.

"Anytime. Now let's scoop Reese up and get him on a plane home. By then, my resources should have a phone number for Malcolm."

Twenty-three

NICK

THEY WERE A couple of blocks from a hotel where he'd stayed with the boys when they'd visited the Detroit auto show so Noah could choose his first car. Nick figured this was Reese's last attempt to find him—stop at the hotel and see if he could pick up Nick's scent. When he hadn't, he'd gone for breakfast.

It was actually in a suburb of Detroit, like almost all the city's best hotels. This suburb had been around for decades and had weathered the economic woes gracefully. The road looked like any other well-to-do suburban street, with people bustling about. Or driving about, as the case was. It wasn't a walking neighborhood. Reese must have walked, though, at least from the hotel, because Nick saw no sign of his car. That got his heart speeding up, even as he knew Reese would rather trek a mile than drive it.

"He's fine," Vanessa murmured, as they waited to cross the road. "There's absolutely no way that Malcolm..."

She trailed off. Nick followed her gaze to see three men getting out of a pickup with Ohio plates. It was the same truck he'd outmaneuvered last night.

"That's not poss—"

She cut herself off and reached to grab Nick's arm, but he already had hers, tugging her back between a truck and a van. Nick double-checked the plate number. There was no question. It was the hunters from last night.

"Stay here," he said. "Cover my back while I go—"

"No. They followed you. They must have. You can't lead them to..."

Again she trailed off. This time, Nick didn't need to track her gaze because they were looking at the same thing—the hunters, as they headed straight for the restaurant.

"How the hell—?" Vanessa began.

"My phone. Somehow they intercepted Reese's call and tracked his cell here. Or they listened in and heard him tell me where he is."

She shook her head. "I'm betting on a supernatural explanation. A clairvoyant on the team or shaman or maybe—"

"It doesn't matter," Nick said. "I'm not standing here until I figure out *how* they found him. They did."

She caught the back of his shirt before he could leave.

"Reese is still fine," she said. "They won't touch him in there."

"I'm—"

"—going in after him. I know. And I won't try to stop you. It's not like I could even if I wanted to. I'm just asking you to take thirty seconds to plan your next move."

"I won't know that until I get in there," he said. "See the layout. See what they're doing."

She nodded. "Fair enough. Swap phones with me then."

He glanced down at her as she held out her cell.

"Take mine so I can contact you," she said. "I'll take yours so I can call Reese and let him know what's going on before you get in there."

Nick handed her his phone. The hunters headed into the restaurant without a backward glance. He followed.

● ● ●

NICK HAD TOLD Vanessa he couldn't formulate a plan until he got the lay of the land. Not entirely true. It was only the specifics he needed more data for. The general plan was simple: get Reese the hell out of there.

Reese didn't look up when Nick walked in, meaning Vanessa had indeed warned him. He sat across the restaurant, drinking a Coke and doing something on his phone—or pretending to. The hunters had taken the booth right behind him. Their heads were together as they talked. They didn't look up either.

Gaze still fixed on his phone, Reese gestured with his free hand. It took a moment for Nick to realize what he was trying to communicate. *Sit down. Wait.*

Nick hesitated, then slid into a booth, positioning himself so he could see Reese but the hunters couldn't see him.

Vanessa's phone pinged. Nick glanced down to see a text from Reese.

They're figuring out how to take me out. Consensus seems to be following me back to my car.

Not surprisingly, then, the hunters didn't know a lot about werewolves—at least not enough to lower their voices.

Nick texted back. *Head to the restroom. I'll confront them. You slip out.*

Reese looked over and mouthed, "Seriously?"

Nick glowered at him. Apparently, he wasn't very good at the expression, because Reese seemed to be stifling a laugh. Reese shook his head and texted.

I'll leave, but only to lure them out. You follow. I'll give them a convenient dark alley to jump me in. We jump them. Find out who they work for.

Nick paused. He could feel Reese watching him.

Another text pinged. *I'm not a kid, Nick. You, me, your spy friend against three of them? Easy odds.*

Nick replied, *It's not them I'm worried about.*

Reese paused, then he sent back, *You saw Malcolm out there?*

No, but he's keeping an eye on the situation. If he's here—

Nick stopped. He didn't send the message. Instead he flipped to send one to his phone, for Vanessa. A simple, *Everything okay?*

His heart pounded as he waited for a reply. When none came after ten seconds, he called. The phone rang. And rang. And went to voice mail.

Nick scrambled out of the booth. It took him all of five seconds to realize what an idiotic move that was. He scrambled up, the hunters spotted him and everybody went still.

The three hunters stood frozen, their mental wheels turning as they figured out their next move. Reese was looking at something across the restaurant. Nick started for the men. Reese swung out of his booth, yelling, "Gun!" and grabbing the nearest hunter by the arm—the arm that was under his jacket, holding his weapon.

The gun flew out. People screamed. Reese grappled with his target, the gun hitting the floor. One of the other hunters just stood there, slack-jawed. The other whipped out his gun.

Nick dove for him as he heard a shout from across the restaurant, "Drop your weapons! Police!"

Nick hit his target as he saw two men jump to their feet. Neither was in uniform, but both had service revolvers trained on the combatants. Detectives. Reese must have spotted the guns or overheard something that gave them away.

Reese gave a werewolf-strength heave and threw his target toward the detectives. Nick was still grappling with his. He snapped the hunter's arm. The man yowled. His gun fell. Nick grabbed him by the jacket and threw him to the cops.

Nick and Reese turned on the third hunter. Behind them, the detectives tried to tell everyone to stand down, drop their weapons, get on the ground, but there was only two of them, busy subduing two big men. The third hunter hadn't pulled a gun, and the detectives seemed to decide Reese and Nick could handle him.

Nick took a slow step toward the hunter. He turned and ran for the back door.

"Bring Vanessa around," Reese said to Nick. "I've got this."

Nick shook his head. "Stay with me. I think Malcolm's here. Vanessa's not answering—"

"Then go get her."

"It could be—"

"—a trap. I know. I'll be careful. But if Malcolm sees me *with* you..."

Reese was right. As much as Nick wanted Reese at his side, he was safer if he wasn't.

"I'll get what I can from that fuckwit," Reese said. "You find Malcolm."

Nick nodded and took off.

● ● ●

MALCOLM HAD BEEN there. Nick could smell him outside. Put that together with Vanessa clearly not being where she should be—or answering her phone—and Nick wasn't pissing around untangling scents to confirm his suspicions. Vanessa would never chase Malcolm if she spotted him. Not after last night. Malcolm must have taken her. And if Nick was going to get her back, he couldn't be crouching on the sidewalk. He needed a shortcut.

He strode into the first empty service lane, found a spot behind a parked delivery van and took off his clothing to begin his Change. Was it the safest spot to do it? Nope. Did he give a shit? Nope.

Nick was never speedy at his Changes, even at the best of times. Unless he was at a Meet, or spending time with Elena and Clay, he rarely did it more than the twice-a-month mini- mum required by Pack law.

The rule was meant to reduce the chance of having a Change come on you at some dangerously inconvenient time, but Nick never had that problem. He did, however, have trouble Changing fast when he needed to, and halfway through, he realized he'd been too hasty, not thinking it through. Would the change in form give him enough advantages to outweigh the delay? He hoped so, because going back now would take just as long.

He finished his Change and struggled up. His legs wobbled, exhausted from the strain, accustomed to a few minutes of rest afterward. He didn't have a few minutes. He closed his eyes and gave himself a muzzle-to-tail shake. There was always some adjustment—to being on four legs, to a black-and-white world, to the sounds and scents that assaulted him from all sides. He snorted, exhaling hard and pawing the ground, getting his bearings as fast as he could.

As he turned to go, Vanessa's phone rang. There was no question of checking it—even if he wasn't in wolf form, he'd shoved his clothing into a recycling bin, under a layer of shredded paper, the phone in his pocket. He did pause, worrying that it was Reese, needing him. Or Vanessa. But he couldn't risk changing back.

The phone stopped ringing. Nick took off.

Twenty-four

VANESSA

VANESSA LISTENED TO her recorded voice, telling the caller to leave a message.

"Nick, it's me. Call back. Please."

She sent the same message by text. There was no reply. It was her own goddamned fault. He'd tried to call her and she'd been running, the phone stuffed in her pocket, unheard.

Now she'd stopped to let Nick know what was going on and discovered she'd had three calls from him. She'd been texting to tell Nick to come after her. Now he was…without knowing what the hell was going on.

Damn it. She really had been out of the field too long.

She looked around the shop. Electronics. She was in the accessories section, catching her breath while pretending to check out the vast selection of earbuds. Malcolm was...well, that was the problem. She wasn't exactly sure where Malcolm was.

She'd spotted him as she'd been waiting on the sidewalk, keeping an eye on the restaurant. *One* eye on the restaurant... while looking for Malcolm. He was using the hunters, not only for amusement and diversion, but to keep tabs on Nick. He'd set them on Nick with that cell phone trick. Now they apparently had their own methods of tracking him, meaning Malcolm could just follow along.

Sure enough, after five minutes, Malcolm had shown up. He'd spotted her almost immediately. Then he'd began circling, like a lone wolf with a deer, scouting out the circumstances, determining the best method of attack.

She hadn't waited for him to figure it out. Take control of the situation. That was what she'd been taught, and that was what she did. She didn't run. He wouldn't have bought that, not only because he must know she wasn't some random woman Nick had picked up, but because, let's face it, with the rental car nearby—and Nick within screaming distance— she'd be an idiot to run.

Earlier, they'd decided that the best trap was an obvious one. Let Malcolm see it. Let his ego take over. So she *had* hurried off—after making it very clear through her body language that she wasn't really fleeing, but was luring him away. In other words, she did exactly what she figured Tina had done, and Malcolm went for it.

Vanessa didn't have Tina's overconfidence, though. Nor that desperate desire to impress Nick. Well, yes, she did want to impress him, but not by taking down Malcolm alone—even if she somehow managed it, he'd think her a reckless fool. She'd stuck to the shop-lined road, where Malcolm wouldn't dare strike. Then she would text Nick, tell him what was happening, and have him in place when she left the shop and found a quiet place where Malcolm would pounce.

Except that obviously wasn't happening because Nick wasn't answering the phone. She tried Reese too, but it went to voice mail. Was he okay? Was Nick with him? Maybe Nick hadn't figured out that an unanswered call meant trouble? Or maybe he'd decided the hunter issue was more pressing.

Damn it. She should have looped him in right away. She hadn't wanted to worry him when he was dealing with the hunters. She figured she could keep Malcolm on the run until Nick was free. Which was, she supposed, exactly what she needed to do now. Keep texting and keep luring—

"Hello."

It was Malcolm Danvers. Standing right beside her.

She would not say he was an attractive man—after how he'd killed Tina and Sharon Stokes, there was no way her brain could see anything attractive there—but she could acknowledge that he'd have no trouble with women. Average height, with a powerful build, blue eyes and dark hair with a sprinkling of gray. All that passed through her brain as simple data, an agent's assessment. What she actually noticed were his eyes. Empty and cold even as they sparkled with amusement at her surprise.

"Oh," he said. "Were you texting Nicky? Telling him where you'll lure me so he can face me down? Please, don't let me interrupt. In fact, I can suggest a place about a block over. Have him meet me there in five minutes. You can stay here…or pretend to stay here while following me to protect your lover." A pause. "He is your lover, I presume?"

She opened her mouth, but he cut her off. "Oh, you're more than *just* his lover, I'm sure. You're one of Rhys Smith's agents. But you're still sleeping with Nicky. That's a given. You're female and reasonably attractive. A little past your prime, but Nicky isn't as choosy as I am. If he doesn't lose his hard-on looking at it, he'll fuck it."

She tried to give no reaction, but she must have, because he laughed. "Sorry to shatter your illusions, my dear. Sleeping with him doesn't mean you're pretty enough for him. You're merely fuckable. For a night. If nothing better presents itself."

He's trying to throw you off balance. And using what he must think every woman is susceptible to—insulting her appearance. Don't stoop to being exactly what he expects.

"Go ahead," he continued. "Text him. Tell him to meet me in the park. It's empty enough."

When she didn't move, he snatched the phone so fast she didn't see it coming. She grabbed for it. He backpedaled, smiling when another customer looked over, startled.

"My phone," he said to the middle-aged man. "You know how wives are. Always 'borrowing' it so they can see what mischief you've been up to."

The man gave a small laugh and continued on his way. Vanessa glanced around. The shop wasn't full, but she'd still cause a scene if she fought Malcolm for the cell.

"Ah, this is *Nicky's* phone." He whistled as he looked at the screen. "I'm surprised it has enough memory to hold his little black book. So many women..." He flipped through. "No notes, though. That's disappointing. Maybe I should forward this list to myself. Rate them for him."

Vanessa grabbed for the phone as he backed up, chuckling.

"One would think you'd appreciate me weeding out the competition." He made a show of flicking down the contact list. "Though even with my appetite, I'm not sure I could make a dent." He looked up. "Such a shame he let you take this, isn't it?"

"A shame?"

"Because it proves he doesn't give a damn. If he did, he'd want to spare your feelings."

"Maybe. Or maybe I already knew how big that list would be and I don't give a shit."

Malcolm smiled, shaking his head. "Don't tell me you didn't take a look. Contacts, e-mail, texts…I'm sure there's some interesting tidbits in there."

"You're right. I should have looked. If you see any tips for what he likes, let me know. Now, is there something else we can discuss, while we both stall, waiting for him to track me here? Opinions on Detroit's prospects for a return to economic stability?"

"No, but I do have an informed opinion on Nick Sorrentino's prospects for a continued existence on this earth. Not good, I fear. In fact, I expect him to leave it in…" He checked his watch. "The next thirty minutes. Probably less, but as you may have realized, he's not the brightest bulb. I have to allow some extra time for him to find us. Killing him, though? That will be quick."

When she didn't reply, he looked over. "Did he tell you I wouldn't kill him because I'm too fond of his father? Let me ask you a question, my dear. Does Antonio know where Nick is?"

Before she could answer, he continued, "I don't require a reply. I know he does not. Antonio was always a poor parent.

Too soft by far. From guilt, after taking Nicky from his mother. He coddled Nicky and made sure nothing in the big, bad world could get him. He still does, I'm sure. If he found out Nicky was coming after me, he'd have chained him in the basement to keep him home. Because Antonio has a secret. Do you know why I left the Pack?"

"Your son beat you out for Alpha."

For one split second, the amused glitter in Malcolm's eyes evaporated. A maelstrom of hate swirled up, so strong and so ugly that Vanessa took an involuntary step back.

"He did not beat me. The coward would never dare challenge me. Not in combat."

"I meant that he was elected over you. The Pack agreed to vote, and he won."

"And do you know why he won? Because Antonio handed him the Alpha crown on a platter. Antonio could coddle Nicky so well because he had plenty of experience at it. From the time my brat was old enough to toddle, Antonio was there, making sure there was nothing sharp or hard for him to fall on. That's the problem with the Sorrentinos. A strong Pack culls the weak. The Sorrentinos embrace them. Protect them. Look at your Nicky, taking in those young mutts. Joey's boy is a half-wit. The other two aren't much better. Misfits and weaklings."

Vanessa was barely listening now. *Just let him rant. Give Nick time to get here.*

195

"Speaking of misfits and weaklings... So my brat fancied himself Alpha, and what did Antonio do? Double-crossed me to hand him the crown. He promised me his vote. Promised me Dennis and Joey's vote. All I had to do was not take my competition out of the race."

Vanessa had to bite her tongue—hard—to keep from saying, *And you bought it?* Antonio's ploy was so obvious that an agent in training wouldn't have fallen for it. But apparently Malcolm had. Or his ego had.

"Antonio double-crossed me. Dennis ran off to Alaska with Joey, and Antonio didn't stop them. That's when I realized he had no intention of giving me his vote. I fought back, but it was too late. The die was cast. The brat got his crown. And me? Well, let's just say I owe Antonio a debt, one I fully intend to repay any minute now. He's about to regret coddling his son when he should have been turning him into a fighter."

"I think you're underestimating Nick."

Malcolm chuckled. "No, I'm quite certain I'm not. He isn't even here yet. The boy can barely follow a well-laid scent. He's no match for me."

"What if he won't fight you?"

"Oh, he will. Did I mention the Sorrentinos have a weakness for weaklings? That includes women. Especially damsels-in-distress."

She laughed. "I'm hardly—"

"Oh, but you will be, as soon as he walks through that door. I'm going to break your spine. Above the first vertebrae. He'll walk in and you'll be on the floor, paralyzed. For life, I'm afraid. It will cause a commotion, naturally, but it will happen too quickly for anyone to react. Nick will see what I've done. I'll run. He'll follow to repay me for my cruelty. Sorrentinos are terribly predictable."

No one could threaten something that terrible so casually, so confidently, warning her, unconcerned that she might actually be able to stop it. He must be bluffing. Only he wasn't. She had only to glance at his face to see that. To glance at his face and then remember Tina and Stokes and the assassin's wife.

She took a moment to steady herself. Then she stepped closer, leaning in to whisper, "You're full of shit."

He turned and met her gaze, smiling. "You keep telling yourself that—"

He stopped as she pressed her weapon into his side.

"A gun, my dear? Really?"

"We're going to walk—"

He kicked her. She wasn't prepared for that. She'd been watching his upper body, ready for him to twist, to grab. Instead he side-kicked her, hard and fast in the calf. As she stumbled, he grabbed for her weapon, only to pull back with a hiss, raising his hand, blood dripping from it.

"Not a gun," she said as she backed away, her knife out.

It took a few moments for customers to figure out what was happening. Even then, it wasn't like pulling out a gun, where everyone screams and panics and dives for cover. Someone would call 911, but otherwise, they just got the hell out of the way, most making a beeline for the door. When neither she nor Malcolm made any effort to stop those fleeing, the rest followed. Since the woman was the one with the knife, obviously no one felt the need to play hero.

"Did you think that was clever?" Malcolm said, waving at the empty store. "A shame, really. You'd have been a good match for Nicky. Equally stupid. Now I don't need to hurt you quickly." He smiled. "I can take my time."

She went for her gun. That was the plan. Clear the shop with the knife. Then pull the gun. Shoot him before the cops arrived. But the moment she went for it, he pounced, anticipating the move. She slashed at him, but she was holding the knife in her left hand now, and it was an awkward, weak slice. It still caught him in the cheek, blade splitting the skin. He didn't even flinch. He hit her knife hand with a chop so hard she thought she heard her wrist snap.

She didn't have time to even process what happened next. That chop to her wrist. Blinding pain. The knife clattering to the floor. And then she was joining it, flat on her stomach. She reacted, her hands slamming down to propel herself up again, but the second she threw her weight on that injured wrist, it buckled and pain ripped through her. Then she felt a foot on her spine and a hand in her hair, ripping it free of the hastily-done twist. Malcolm yanked her head back so far she yelped.

"I can snap your neck and kill you," he said. "Or break your spine and paralyze you. Choose."

She reached back with her uninjured hand, her fingers blazing, but he was wise enough to stay clear of her fire. She had to get her gun—

She couldn't. His foot pinned her to the floor with her gun crushed beneath her.

You were a fool, she thought. *An absolute fool. You knew what he was capable of. You thought you were prepared for it. You weren't.*

"Choose," he said. "You have five seconds or I'll rip your scalp from your head, and then I'll crush your spine. Then I'll see how much *more* amusement I can have before Nicky arrives. Do you want to live paralyzed? Or die?"

"Live," she said quickly. "I want to live."

"Beg."

Her mouth opened, and then shut. He wasn't going to let her live. He just wanted her to beg and then, when she thought her life spared, he'd snap her neck.

"Beg or I—"

A scream sounded from the back rooms. Malcolm tensed, and though she couldn't see him, she knew he was looking over his shoulder. She grabbed her hair, wrenching it from his grip as she rolled from under him. There was a commotion in the back, but he ignored it and knocked her to the floor. She went for her gun, but in the time it would take her to pull it, he could pin her. She'd lost. There was no way out of this. Nothing to do but her job. Her mission. Finish that and accept whatever came next.

She reached into her pocket and pushed the panic button.

Twenty-five

NICK

NICK HAD FOLLOWED the path easily enough. At first, when it became clear that Vanessa was actually leading Malcolm—their paths had diverged enough that he couldn't be forcing her somewhere—Nick had been confused. She wouldn't run, not when Nick had been right across the road. Once he realized Vanessa's trail stuck to the sidewalk, he understood her plan—lure Malcolm along an occupied street until he could catch up. She must have been the one who called, to tell him her plan.

So he was no longer barreling down the road, certain she was five seconds from a terrible death. He did lope along the sidewalk, though. As a wolf. In a Detroit suburb. Elena would throttle him. Clay would help. Under the circumstances, though, there was nothing else he could do. There were no alleys. No maze of side streets and service lanes. This was it—a major suburban thoroughfare in daylight. He could tell himself it wasn't so bad, and the shopping district wasn't exactly packed. But even if people would only report seeing a huge dark brown dog, he was still in serious shit.

He made good time, if that helped. And once the trail went into the electronics store, he did keep to the service lane that ran along the side and back, pacing as he figured out his next move.

Vanessa had Malcolm cornered, so to speak, though he doubted Malcolm would agree. Malcolm was, however, unable to kill her in such a public place. They were at a stand off, as Vanessa waited for Nick. No, as she waited for *human* Nick, with hands that could open the goddamned door.

He could Change back, but that would take too much time, too long when he'd be useless, caught between forms. There was only one option: let Vanessa know he was there. That meant letting her see him. He walked down the service lane, planning to pace in front of the store. Just as he headed there, though, a commotion sounded inside. No screams, thankfully, but sudden chatter, rapid footsteps, the front door opening, then more footsteps as people spilled onto the sidewalk.

Nick raced to the sidewalk. The store was emptying fast. People weren't running panicked, though. They were just getting the hell out of there. Meaning Malcolm had made his move.

Nick ran to the front door, but by the time he reached it, everyone was gone and it was closed tight. He tore around the back. Someone would come out there, an employee or a customer. But the door stayed closed. He strained to hear noises from inside. Nothing. He tried to take comfort in that. Vanessa had her gun. If Malcolm did anything, she'd shoot him. Whatever was happening, it couldn't be that dire. Yet his heart hammered as he paced, desperately struggling for an idea.

Break the front window. No, get a look through that window. Evaluate the situation. Break it if needed.

He was turning to start down the lane again when the rear door creaked open. He crouched, waiting and watching as the door slowly opened and then—

Nick shot forward. A young clerk let out a shriek. Nick knocked him flying and scrambled through the open door. He raced along the narrow back hall, knocking over everything in his path. Finally he saw the half-open door to the shop floor ahead.

Nick smacked the door open with his muzzle and charged through. Then he saw them, grappling on the floor. It was no contest. Malcolm was only trying to get his grip and as soon as he found it...

As Nick raced over, they both stopped. Vanessa's elbow shot up, slamming Malcolm in the jaw. It was enough to make him fall back. He could have recovered and pinned her, but Nick was barreling straight at them, and as arrogant as Malcolm was, he wasn't about to ignore a charging wolf. As Vanessa struggled up, reaching for her gun, Malcolm gave her a shove. Then he ran.

Malcolm tore around a display and made a beeline for the rear door. Nick glanced back at Vanessa.

"Go!" she said. "I've called them. They're coming. I'll lead them to you."

He took off after Malcolm.

● ● ●

A HEALTHY EGO is a wonderful thing. An overinflated one, though? That gets you into trouble. Antonio had taught Nick that, clamping down whenever he got a little too cocky about the numerous gifts life had bestowed on him.

Malcolm's ego failed him almost as soon as he got out that rear door. He should have run for the street. That was his only chance. Nick might break the rules enough to race along it in wolf form at midday, but he'd never take down Malcolm there. He'd need to stick to back roads and hope to drive Malcolm to a more suitable place.

But running to the safety of humans was more than Malcolm's ego could bear. He tore along the service lane until he neared the end. Then he grabbed a fire escape ladder. He was ten feet up when Nick sprinted and leaped. He'd been aiming to grab Malcolm by the back of the shirt but that, he realized, had been a bit of ego on his own part. He managed to snag Malcolm's foot. He clamped down hard, though, and when he dropped, Malcolm dropped with him.

They fought. Nick hadn't Changed just so he could better track Malcolm—he knew being in wolf form was the only way he'd get the upper hand in a fight. Malcolm didn't concede easily, though. Nick tore at him with fang and claw, ripping through fabric and flesh, and still Malcolm fought, kicking and punching, aiming for Nick's stomach, eyes, muzzle, all the sensitive spots. Soon Nick was fighting through a haze of pain and blood.

He could lose this fight. He hadn't considered that. A fight between a wolf and an unarmed man clearly favored the beast. But Malcolm was on a whole other level, and it wasn't just martial superiority. He was fighting for his life and it seemed to numb him against every injury.

When Malcolm's fist connected with the side of Nick's skull, hitting a spot he'd already pummeled, the pain of that sledgehammer drive knocked Nick unconscious. It was only a second's dip into blackness before he yanked himself out, but it would have been enough for Malcolm to get free. Escape and run. Instead, he grabbed Nick's muzzle and tried to break his neck. And it was then that Nick realized Malcolm wasn't the only one fighting for his life.

Malcolm meant to kill him. The shock of that realization almost made Nick laugh. Had he really doubted it? After what Malcolm had done to Tina and the Stokes? Yes, he had, because no matter how hard he tried to convince Vanessa of Malcolm's lethality, he'd considered himself exempt.

He was not exempt. And that was, it turned out, exactly the motivation he needed to dig deeper, fight harder. He clawed and snapped and threw himself into the fight as he never had before, and when he finally got Malcolm pinned, it came almost as a shock. But he was upright and Malcolm was on his back and Nick had his jaws around Malcolm's throat.

One chomp. That's all it would take, and the most dangerous wolf the Pack had ever known would be vanquished. By the omega wolf. Yet Nick didn't think for a moment how sweet that would be. How fittingly ignoble an end. He thought only of his duty. His mission was to find Malcolm. Not to kill him. That right belonged to Clay. Yet he could not let Malcolm go. Clay wouldn't want that. Yes, Clay would love to kill the bastard himself, but ending Malcolm's life—by any means—was more important.

Nick pulled back for the killing bite. As he swung down, he saw the look in Malcolm's eyes. The rage. The shame. The humiliation. And yes, it was sweet.

Then he heard a shout. Vanessa. That stopped him mid-lunge. Malcolm tried to buck up, but Nick had him firmly pinned. Another shout. A different voice now. Not so much a shout as a snarl of rage.

Clay.

Something hit Nick in the shoulder and for a moment, he thought it was Clay, and confusion flashed through him.

I was doing the right thing. I wasn't stealing your kill. I—

That's when he heard the shot, as if his brain delayed processing it. He heard the shot and then another, and shouts and bellows of rage and fear.

Nick had been shot.

Malcolm reared up again. Nick tried to hold him, but Malcolm managed to chop him in the shoulder, where the bullet had penetrated, and it was too much. Nick staggered enough for Malcolm to scramble out from under him.

Malcolm ran. Nick tried to follow, but his injured shoulder gave way. He glanced back. Clay, Elena and Reese were running toward him, as Vanessa, Jayne and Rhys subdued two men with guns—more werewolf hunters, he presumed. They were still fifty feet back, not much beyond the shop door. Malcolm was escaping. Nick lurched after him, but couldn't manage more than a hobbling lope.

"Stay there!" Elena said, racing up, in the lead. "We've got this. Reese? Stay with Nick. Get that bleeding under control."

Reese slowed. Elena and Clay raced past him, but Nick knew it was too late. Malcolm was gone. They'd lost him.

Twenty-six

NICK

THEY WERE IN a hotel room—Nick, Elena, Clay, Reese, Vanessa and Rhys. Jayne had already departed with backup to recover Tina's body. Rhys had bound Vanessa's wrist at the scene—it was sprained not broken. Then they'd grabbed food, and the werewolves were now ripping through it as if they hadn't eaten in weeks.

Vanessa and Rhys watched them, bemused, as if wondering how anyone could have an appetite after the last few hours. But it was precisely that close call that gave them the appetite. This was a celebration. Yes, as Nick predicted, Malcolm had escaped. But they hadn't lost him. He was right there, a blip on a screen, tracked by the microchip Vanessa had implanted during their fight. It was the best on the market—the black market, that is—the kind of tech the CIA would insist didn't even exist. And the kind of tech Malcolm was never going to find with all his cuts and gouges.

Elena was in charge of the tracking box. Rhys turned it over as he took Vanessa off to talk shop, leaving the were-wolves to finish their meal.

"If you keep checking that, you'll start seeing blips in your sleep," Reese said, as Elena glanced at the device for the hundredth time.

"Just making sure it doesn't stop until he's in the next state."

"Unless it stops because he's decided to give up," Clay said through a mouthful of burger. "Save us the trouble and off himself, unable to live with the humiliation."

"Of nearly dying at my hands?" Nick said.

"Of nearly dying at the hands of anyone he considers his inferior, which goes for 99.9 percent of the population."

"You don't need to qualify that. Getting killed by me would have been the worst possible fate. I could see it in his eyes. He was pissed."

Clay grinned. "Yeah, I noticed that even from where I was. Looked good on him. Too bad those moron bounty hunters interfered. Would have been a fitting end for Malcolm Danvers."

"Oh, I don't know," Elena said, stealing a handful of fries from Clay. "I think living with the humiliation for a while will be even better. He knows Nick had him. He was saved by happenstance. That's going to sting for a long time."

"Right into his afterlife," Clay said. "Which will come soon."

"So what's next?" Reese asked.

"Next we let him get comfortable," Elena said. "Lower his guard. This little tracker means we don't need to worry about him coming after any of the Pack. If he sets foot in New York State, we'll take him down. Otherwise, I'll track him until he figures he's safe. Then Clay and I will take a well-deserved vacation."

"Culminating in the death of Malcolm Danvers," Clay said.

"And the hunters?" Reese asked. He'd interrogated the one he'd chased and gotten contact information for the guy setting the bounties.

Elena chewed a fry before answering. The hunters were a nuisance, to be sure. Possibly a deadly one. But Malcolm was deadlier.

"I can take that," Nick said. "Pay the guy a visit. Convince him it's not a good idea to put out bounties on us."

"I'll run backup," Reese said. "We might even get Morgan to come along. He should be home by then."

Elena looked at Nick. "You sure?"

"I can handle it."

She met his gaze. "I wasn't asking that. Obviously you can handle it. But Karl's up on the duty roster. I can send him if you want a break."

"Nah, I'm on it already. I might as well stay on it. Compared to hunting Malcolm, this should be a breeze."

"Famous last words," Clay said.

Nick laughed, and they continued plowing through the meal.

• • •

MALCOLM HAD INDEED vacated the state. Heading west. Far west. Licking his wounds. Clay and Elena had already left, eager to get back before the kids returned that evening.

Nick was riding back with Reese. First, they dropped Rhys and Vanessa off at the airport. Nick hadn't had a moment alone with Vanessa since that morning, so he accompanied her into the terminal, carrying her bag so she wouldn't strain her wrist. Once inside, Rhys went off to buy the tickets.

"You're going to stop at Stonehaven, right?" Vanessa said. "Let Jeremy take a look at your shoulder when he gets home tonight?"

"I am, though I'm sure he'll say that Rhys's first-aid job is all it needs. That and some rest. Werewolves heal fast."

She nodded and hoisted her purse. "Okay..."

"I'd like to see you again."

She smiled. "To cash that rain check?"

He laughed. "No. Well, yes, but I'd just...I'd like to see you again."

"I could come along and help you fix this werewolf bounty mess."

"Ah. Okay. I'll take the hint. I know you're trying to be nice, but you can just say no. You wanted a fling. I understand that—"

She cut him off with a kiss, laughing when he started in surprise.

"Sorry," she said. "I couldn't resist. I definitely want to see you again, Nick. If we make it dinner, though, then we have to figure out where to meet and who travels, and it becomes this big production, with expectations and pressure and…" She made a face. "General awkwardness. I'm too old for that. But I would like to spend more time with you, see what happens. I think the best way we can do that is to work together on another case."

"We could do that."

"Is that a yes?"

He leaned down and kissed her. "Yes."